Crawling Back To Start

Greg Starypan

Copyright © 2014 Greg Starypan
All rights reserved.

ISBN-10: 1495429253
ISBN-13: 9781495429255
Library of Congress Control Number: 2014903629
CreateSpace Independent Publishing Platform
North Charleston, South Carolina

For Artie, Art, and Donna

ACKNOWLEDGMENTS

I want to extend my heartfelt thanks to my good friend Don Wilder. He was my sounding board from the very beginning and had the thankless task of reading the earliest passages of my book when my writing style was as green and undeveloped as a freshly bottled barleywine. It was Don who provided me with constructive criticism and encouraged me to experiment until I found my narrative voice. His criticism was always insightful, delicately conveyed and dead on the mark.

He was also the one who introduced me to the beautiful flute music of Coyote Oldman. I listened to this spiritually uplifting music for hours as I commuted to and from work on the train and tried to write. I believe it helped me find my narrative voice. It became my soundtrack as I wrote.

I also want to acknowledge the fine work of Shannon Carson, who served as the copy editor of this manuscript. Her corrections, comments, and suggestions improved my work, and without her careful scrutiny, this book would not be as error-free as it is.

If you like this book, it is, in part, because of Don's and Shannon's contributions.

ONE

Those closest to him called him Tirebiter, or Biter, for short. An old friend had given him this nickname years' earlier but had never bothered to explain his inspiration for the moniker. As a result, no one really knew its derivation. Some thought it was a reference to a mutt that at one time had been the unofficial student mascot at USC. Others assumed that it came from a character immortalized in the records of a 1960s comedy troupe called Firesign Theater. However, given Biter's known affinity for beer, the story that gained the widest acceptance was that he obtained the nickname one night when, as a college freshman, he attended a kegger and was subsequently found drunk and passed out in a fraternity parking lot, hugging the front tire of a 1963 Corvette. His roommate, who ended up carrying him back to the dorm, supposedly had claimed Biter was so disheveled and pathetic that he looked like a mongrel dog, biting the car's whitewalls when he found him. Suffice it to say, that although Biter was initially uncomfortable with the nickname, the sobriquet stuck to him like gum on the bottom of a shoe and, over time, he actually came to embrace it.

It was closing time at the zoo where Biter worked as an animal keeper. As a security guard traveled the grounds in a golf cart, reminding visitors that it was now time for them to exit, Biter sat at his desk in the behind-the-scenes keeper's area, watching a wild-caught wolverine on a video monitor as it frantically tried to escape from the exhibit to which it had been introduced just hours earlier.

With saliva clinging tenaciously to its muzzle, the wolverine panted heavily as it made yet another attempt to scale the gunite wall that separated it from freedom. Biter could hear the creature's labored breathing and sense its desperation. He marveled at the animal's brute strength as he watched it attempt to scale the near vertical wall. Pound for pound, the wolverine was undoubtedly the strongest animal he had ever encountered. His respect for this largest terrestrial member of the weasel family made it even more difficult for him to witness its repeated failures.

With eight years of experience as a keeper, he had witnessed this sad scenario countless times with a whole host of animals, but it had never impacted him this way before. For some reason, Biter felt a visceral connection to this one wolverine and found himself rooting for it to succeed, but he knew there was no way this creature—no matter how strong—could defy the law of gravity and make it past the severe overhang that mushroomed out over the top of the exhibit. He felt like a young kid, witnessing the defeat of his first hero, and coming to the sad, sobering realization that the object of his adulation was not invincible but a mere mortal, with weaknesses and flaws, like everyone else.

Although Biter would never have admitted it, the fact that he had just broken up with his girlfriend Cassandra the week before played heavily on his mind and was largely the cause of his newfound angst. Perhaps he subconsciously related the wolverine's struggle to escape confinement as an allegory of his own efforts to avoid marriage, and maybe this was the reason for his empathy. He had lived with his girlfriend for over two years, and they had never had any problems, at least not until she started to pressure him to tie the knot. He had made it exceedingly clear from the very beginning of their relationship that he wasn't interested in marriage, and he had thought that they had an understanding. Cassandra was originally good about letting him have his freedom, but she had become increasingly critical of the amount of time he spent with his friends in their local tavern. She was tired of waiting for him to settle down, and he was tired of her nagging. She had given him the ultimatum to either make a commitment or leave.

Since she knew the thought of marriage scared him, he felt she had really left him with no choice but to move out. He was adamant that he would not slowly surrender his independence the way so many of his friends had just to maintain a relationship. If a woman was really in love with him, he reasoned, she should accept him as is—flaws and all—and not have this overriding need to mold him into her version of the perfect male.

Watching the wolverine's struggle to escape only reinforced the subconscious parallels Biter saw in his own situation. He knew he couldn't sit idly by and do nothing. He grabbed one of the large, live traps that were stacked in one corner of the room and placed it on the food prep table. He then opened a large can of dog food and placed it inside the trap. From inside the keeper's area, he lifted a cable, which opened a stainless steel, guillotine door that provided access from the adjacent exhibit into the animal's behind-the-scenes holding pen. He did this so that the animal would have a place to retreat when he entered the exhibit. With the trap in one hand, he unlocked the door that opened into the exhibit and entered the enclosure.

As Biter had anticipated—since the wolverine wasn't cornered—it didn't challenge him. Instead, it ran frantically around the perimeter of the exhibit, looking for an avenue of escape. Upon finding the opening that led into the holding pen, the animal retreated to the safety of the open den box. Biter then set the live trap and exited the enclosure. When he reentered the keeper's room, the wolverine immediately ran back into the exhibit.

Biter returned to his desk and trained his eyes on the video monitor. For at least an hour or more, he watched to see if the wolverine would be lured into the trap. Although he had already seen the paperwork that accompanied the animal, he could have told you much about the animal just by looking at it now. Based on its size, it was obviously a male. At the shoulders, it was the height of a standard cocker spaniel, but much more robust in build. It looked like a small bear with a luxurious coat of russet-brown fur. Its most noticeable feature was its huge, oversized paws. Like snowshoes, these broad, fur-covered feet enabled the animal to travel over deep snow unencumbered. The fact that it walked flat-footed made it even more bear-like in appearance.

But unlike a bear, the wolverine had two blonde stripes, running from its shoulders laterally down the sides of its back, which were reminiscent of a smaller, but more familiar member of the weasel clan, the skunk. Like all members of its family, the wolverine had scent glands that were used to mark its territory and signal its presence to females, but, unlike the skunk, its musk glands weren't used as a means of defense.

As Biter watched the wolverine pace back and forth in the exhibit, he recalled that among its many common names was "skunk bear." He couldn't think of a more appropriate nickname for this mammal.

The animal's jet black eyes and muzzle contrasted sharply with its forehead and temples, which were silver-gray in color. While this could mistakenly lead the average person to assume this was an old animal, Biter knew this was far from the truth. He had worked with enough wolverines to know that the light-colored facial mask was quite common and that this animal was young, robust and in his prime.

His heart sank each time the creature encountered the trap and ignored the food. Just as he was about to give up and return the animal to the security of its holding pen, the wolverine stopped pacing and appeared to take interest in the food.

Biter held his breath as he watched the wolverine slowly enter the trap. The animal's tentativeness was unnerving. Would the wolverine spook and jet backwards, or continue its agonizingly sluggish pace forward? The suspense was killing him. Suddenly, the animal tripped the food pan, and the doors of the trap came crashing down. He had him!

Biter grabbed a blanket out of the closet in the keeper's room and quickly entered the exhibit. He knew the animal would initially try to claw and bite its way out of the trap, and he didn't want the animal to injure itself in the process. As he ran toward the trap, the wolverine became even more agitated. Biter quickly placed the blanket over the cage, and the animal almost immediately began to calm down. He waited for the wolverine's vociferous growls to subside to a few, infrequent, half-hearted, guttural sounds.

When he was confident that the animal had accepted its fate and wouldn't bloody its paws trying to escape, Biter retrieved a hand cart from the keeper's office, loaded the blanket-draped trap onto it and wheeled it out the back door of his office to the service area where his rusty Ford Ranger was parked. The trap with the animal proved to be a heavy load, and he struggled to lift it into the bed of his truck.

Closing the canopy, Biter jumped inside the cab, started the engine and backed out of his parking stall. He then drove to the zoo's perimeter fence, grabbed the remote on his dashboard and depressed the button to open the gate. As he waited for the fence to open, Biter stared at his reflection in the rear-view mirror. His dark brown eyes were expressionless. He knew he was about to commit an act that would surely get him fired and could likely land him in prison for theft, yet his eyes betrayed no emotion. He winced as he recalled one of Cassandra's verbal barbs from their recent break-up. "We're about to end something that could be so right for both of us," she said, "and yet, you look like your reading *The New York Times*. You're afraid to show your emotions. You're afraid it makes you vulnerable."

Not wanting to confront the truth, Biter diverted his gaze from the mirror and noticed that the zoo's perimeter gate was now wide open. Stepping on the accelerator pedal, he drove past the gate, depressed the remote once again, and watched in his rear-view mirror as the fence slowly closed behind him. As he left the zoo's grounds and navigated the dusty, serpentine Forest Service roads that would eventually lead him to his chosen release site, the unmistakable odor of a road-killed skunk permeated the cab of his vehicle. Rather than finding the fetid scent offensive, Biter actually embraced the familiar odor. It served as an olfactory taxi, transporting him back to a time when he was a freshman zookeeper. He laughed to himself as he remembered how gullible and eager to please he was at this stage in his development.

One of the zoo's elderly volunteers had caught a spotted skunk in a homemade live trap. She thought it would be a good addition to the zoo's Forest Animals exhibit, and Biter had readily agreed. In addition to wolverines, the zoo had several other representatives of the weasel family—long-tailed weasels, badgers and river otters, but no skunks—the members of the weasel family with the most highly developed, anal scent glands.

As he remembered it now, the woman had lived about an hour away from the zoo, but only about fifteen minutes from his apartment. To him, it made no sense to drive out to the zoo to get a company vehicle and then backtrack to retrieve the animal. Since he didn't own a truck at that time, he borrowed one from a nearby friend but neglected to tell him what it was that he would be transporting.

When Biter arrived at the old lady's home, he saw that her trap was made out of scrap lumber. By the looks of it, he guessed the trap had been fashioned from an old wooden pallet. The slats fit together rather loosely, and, as a result, the interior of the trap was not entirely dark, and the animal could see out. As he threw a blanket over the trap in an effort to darken its interior and calm the animal, the skunk let go with a pungent, sulfurous salvo. From that moment on, the trap, the blanket, Biter, and the truck were soiled goods.

He recalled with amusement the moment he returned the vehicle to his friend. No words were exchanged, and none were needed. The look on his buddy's face spoke volumes. Biter knew it would be a cold day in hell before he would ever again be able to borrow his friend's truck or anything else of his for that matter.

Biter then traveled to the supermarket, purchased several gallon containers of tomato juice, drove home and bathed in it in an attempt to rid his body of the relentless, malodorous scent. He laughed hysterically now as he relived the moment in his mind's eye. His bathroom, he thought, must have looked like the shower scene from the movie, *Psycho*, and his apartment for weeks probably smelled like rotten eggs!

As Biter drove deeper and deeper into the forest, he encountered a whole host of animals along the way. A cottontail stood motionless until his truck was nearly upon it. Only at the last minute did it scurry across the road in front of his vehicle as if on a kamikaze mission.

A ruffed grouse, eating gravel on the roadside, at first remained motionless and then exploded in a flurry of wings as it sought cover in a nearby thicket.

Further on, a Douglas tree squirrel, perched securely on a branch of a western red cedar, scolded him incessantly as he rounded a curve in the road and invaded its territory.

The frequency of these potential prey encounters was reassuring for it gave Biter the confidence that the animal he was about to release would have no problem finding food. He knew wolverines were legendary for subduing quarry far larger than themselves. He was aware of one documented case where a wolverine actually took down a moose—albeit one that was mired in deep snow—and another case, where one drove a bear off an elk carcass it had claimed as its own.

The Forest Service road Biter was traveling terminated in a grassy clearing dominated by a few dead snags with moss-covered limbs. Red alders were reclaiming the perimeter but had not yet obliterated the view out over the top of the ridge. Biter could see the evening fog, slowly blanketing the distant hills as it slowly descended towards the valley floor. Shafts of the setting sun found their way through the trees.

Biter opened up the canopy of his truck, dragged the heavy blanket-draped cage to the tailgate and slowly lowered it to the ground. As if on cue, the wolverine came to life and began clawing and biting the trap in an effort to escape. Biter waited for the animal to calm down. He then opened the cage to release it. Expecting the wolverine to explode from the trap, he braced himself for its exit. Instead, there was no response. Seconds turned to minutes, and just as he started to relax his guard, the animal sprang from the cage and ran hell bent for the trees.

To Biter, the perfect scenario would have been for the wolverine to run towards the edge of the clearing and then stop and turn to make eye contact with its liberator before continuing on its path to freedom. It was as if he wanted, or needed, some spiritual validation that releasing this animal was the right thing to do.

Instead, the wolverine reached the perimeter of the trees and never looked back. Biter was deflated and felt cheated. He had committed what he considered a selfless act and, in his mind, had received no gratification for his good deed. For a few more minutes, he stared at the last place he had seen the wolverine disappear into the trees. He then lifted the trap and returned it to his vehicle.

As he climbed inside the cab, he was tempted to once again check out his countenance in the rear-view mirror. Feeling apprehensive and a bit confused, he thought better of it and turned the mirror down toward the dash. He started the truck, turned the vehicle around and headed back to the zoo to return the cage. As he made the long trek down the winding, dirt road, the sun made its descent behind the surrounding hills. Biter switched on his headlights, knowing that it would be a long trip back with nothing but darkness and his second thoughts to accompany him. He turned on his CD player and hoped that some good music would raise his spirits.

TWO

The next morning, Biter unlocked the door to the keeper's kitchen and saw Wes Cleveland, a co-worker, cutting up fruits and vegetables and placing allotted portions of each in stainless steel pans on the table. Wes was a large, overweight man with a thinning mane of curly white, shoulder-length hair and a full, pure-white beard. Although the company-issued, slate-gray, ranger shirt and dark green pants he currently wore were not the traditional attire one would associate with Santa Claus, the man was a dead ringer for this cultural icon. Wes routinely dressed up as Santa for the employees' Christmas parties and portrayed him in the zoo's public events during the holiday season. Biter had no doubt that an uninitiated observer, coming upon the scene, would guess he had caught jolly Ol' St. Nick preparing food for his reindeer. In reality, Wes was in the process of preparing the daily rations for the herbivores in the zoo's Forest Animals exhibit.

Biter noticed that Wes, as usual, was wearing a tie-dye "T" underneath his ranger shirt. Only the neck of the multi-colored T-shirt was visible, but he understood it was Wes's subtle protest of the zoo's dress policy and an expression of his individualism. Biter knew his friend was a die-hard Grateful Dead fan and guessed these shirts were souvenirs from the many concerts he had attended over the years.

"You're in a lot of trouble," Wes said. "I don't know if you're aware of it or not, but the new wolverine you were introducing into the exhibit yesterday has escaped. The Acting Prez is looking for you and has called here several times to see if you were in yet. I'm supposed to tell you to report to his office as soon as you get in. If I were you, I'd hightail it up to the man's office."

Biter patted Wes on the back. "Thanks, friend. I'm on my way."

"No," Wes said, as he dropped his knife and grabbed Biter by the arm. "I don't think you understand. This is serious. Something's up. Eddie Haskell is looking for a scapegoat here, and, right now, you seem to be the only one with a target on your back."

Eddie Haskell was the nickname Biter had given the zoo's Acting President, James Dressel, several years earlier when he was still second in command and serving as the zoo's Director of Finance. Like the disingenuous teen character from the 1950s television series, *Leave It To Beaver*—who was infamous for his transparent attempts to ingratiate himself with the adult characters on the show—Dressel also used obsequious flattery as a way to curry favor with his superiors. Biter found this behavior repugnant and became almost apoplectic in staff meetings when Dressel would stoop so low as to quote the President verbatim, as if his words were pearls of wisdom deserving of some special reverence.

Whenever Dressel did this in a staff meeting, Biter would lean over to whichever zookeeper was sitting next to him and whisper what was probably the fictional Eddie Haskell's best known line of dialogue, "Oh, that's a lovely dress you're wearing this evening, Mrs. Cleaver." It never failed to get a laugh from his co-workers because they knew it was his way of saying Dressel was a toady. The other keepers, sharing Biter's disdain for the man, had been quick to adopt the nickname, and it was still widely used by them even now in their personal conversations.

Biter looked Wes directly in his eyes to reassure him that he had his undivided attention. "How can I hightail it up to the man's office if you don't let go of me?"

"I'm just worried about you," Wes said as he released his hold on Biter's arm. "It's no secret that there's no love lost between you two. Don't get me wrong, we're all on your side, at least all of the keepers that is. We hate that little shit as much as you do, but he's got the office now—at least on an interim basis—and that gives him the advantage."

Wes's words sunk in, and Biter decided he needed to prepare himself for how he would react should his meeting with Dressel go badly. Biter gave his friend a hug. "Wes, you really are a dear friend, and I do appreciate your concern."

As Biter started for the door, Wes blurted out the question he had told himself he wouldn't ask, "Gosh, darn it. I have to know. Did you do it?"

Biter pretended to not understand the question. "Do what?"

"Did you have a hand in the wolverine's escape?"

"Now why would I do a bone-headed thing like that?"

"I haven't been able to come up with a reason that makes any sense," Wes said honestly. "I probably know you better than anybody else here. A while back, I would have said there was no way you could have done such a thing. You were always the consummate professional. But I have to say, you've been kind of squirrelly the past week or so since you and your girl broke up. Please don't take offense. I love you like one of my sons. I hope you know that. I guess I'm just asking if you're OK."

"No offense taken," Biter said as he headed for the door. "I'm fine."

Wes watched him leave. "You still haven't answered my question," he pleaded.

Biter wanted to tell his friend the truth, but he knew if he did, and Wes were asked to testify in court, his friend would be confronted with the thankless choice of either lying under oath or testifying against him. He didn't want to put his friend in this position, so he feigned ignorance. "I don't know what you mean. I answered your question. I said I was OK." With that, Biter exited the kitchen and headed for the President's office.

Biter and Dressel had butted heads from the very beginning, and, as Wes had said, it was common knowledge amongst the staff that the two men hated each other. To Biter, Dressel was a small man, not because of his stature—since he and Dressel were both short and of roughly the same height—but because the Acting President was small by every other measure of a man. He was an insecure individual who tried to hide his inferiority complex by being excessively authoritarian. He was petty and vindictive and didn't know the first thing about loyalty. He took credit for other people's hard work but assumed none of the blame when mistakes were made. If a good employee got on his bad side for some reason, no matter how inconsequential the infraction, he'd target this person and eventually find an excuse to fire him. Yet, at the same time, he'd blatantly reward unexceptional employees who stroked his ego. In Biter's mind, Dressel got where he was by sucking up to his superiors, not because he was a skilled administrator. He found it humorous, and more than a bit ironic, that now that Dressel was in charge—and there was no one else's ass to kiss—the man was out of his element and didn't have a clue about what to do.

Biter, in comparison, was self-confident, fiercely independent, and intensely loyal to his friends. If he had an Achilles' heel, it was that he was brutally honest, and his facial expressions were incapable of hiding his true feelings. If he liked you, you could sense it immediately, and if he didn't, his disdain was equally transparent. Dressel could tell by the look on Biter's face that he had no respect for him. He had also heard rumors that Biter frequently mocked him at the local tavern when the keepers gathered there to have a few beers after work. This just fed Dressel's paranoia and made him hate Biter even more.

Upon entering the Administration Building, Biter bounded up the steps to the President's office and greeted the receptionist. "Good morning, Maggie," he said, as he scooped some M&M's from the bowl she had on her desk. "You're as lovely as always."

Maggie was a winsome beauty in her mid-twenties. Of Scottish descent, she had long auburn hair pulled back in a bun, hazel eyes and fair skin. "Oh, you are a charmer," she joked. She glanced over at the President's open door to be sure he wasn't within earshot and then leaned across the desk and lowered her voice. "Be careful," she whispered. "He's in a miserable mood today. He's already snapped at me several times for no apparent reason...and he likes me."

"Oh, come on, Maggie," Biter whispered teasingly. "You know everybody loves me."

Maggie giggled, "What have you been smoking? You know how that vein always pops out on his forehead when he gets excited or upset?"

Biter nodded affirmatively.

"Well, it's really noticeable today," she said. "And, quite frankly, you seem to have a way of bringing this characteristic out in him, so be on your best behavior."

"Aren't you going to call him to let him know I'm here?" Biter asked.

"No, he told me to send you right in when you arrived."

"OK, then," Biter replied. "I guess I'd better make my entrance. Wish me luck."

"You'll need it," Maggie said sadly.

Biter stood at the entryway to the office and knocked briefly on the doorjamb. Dressel immediately looked up from his laptop. "Oh, it's you. Come in. Close the door and take a seat."

Dressel was a delicate-looking man with short-cropped, black hair. His complexion had a pinkish hue, which Biter thought looked remarkably similar to the skin of a hairless lab rat. He was always impeccably dressed. From the first time Biter set eyes on the man, he felt that Dressel was out of place in both his environment and his time. Dressel's penchant for wearing a suit and tie was more fitting for Wall Street than the zoo community, and his prissy demeanor was better suited for a different century. Biter could easily imagine Dressel, dressed in a satin waistcoat and wearing a powdered wig, listening to Mozart's sonatas. He found it impossible to envision him, dressed in blue jeans and a T-shirt, working at a blue-collar job or drinking beers with his bros.

The oversized, oak desk Dressel hid behind seemed to swallow him up and made him look smaller than his actual size. Biter fought back a grin for he knew Dressel thought the large desk made him look important. In reality, the expansive desk made him look like a kid playing grown-up in his father's office.

Dressel waited for Biter to get seated. "We have a problem here. It seems the new wolverine you were introducing into the exhibit has escaped. I'm told the holding pen's guillotine door was left open."

Biter knew whatever story he came up with would have to be rock solid or he would be out of a job, or, even worse, be on his way to jail. "I'm sorry if I forgot to close the gate," Biter said apologetically. "But that would have only given the animal access into the exhibit. The wolverine would still have had to scale the walls to escape. No animal has ever done that in this exhibit, so I'm at a loss to explain how it got away. The only thing I can figure was that this was an exceptional animal."

"Exceptional in what way? Perhaps the animal sprouted wings and flew out of the exhibit. Could that be it?"

"I thought this was supposed to be a serious discussion," Biter replied in annoyance. "Exceptional in the sense that it was an extremely robust animal, and, unlike many of the animals we've received, it hadn't been in captivity very long. Its hunger for freedom would be greater. I would think this would be a powerful motivator."

Biter watched as Dressel tapped his fingers nervously on his desk. "What would you say if I told you one of our security guards said he saw you last night, hauling something out of the zoo on a hand cart?"

"I would say I was just taking out garbage to the dumpster," Biter said matter-of-factly.

"Look, I'm not going to pull any punches here. I think you had a hand in the animal's escape. If I could prove it, I wouldn't be wasting my time talking to you. You'd be telling your story to the police. I know in my gut that you're guilty, but I can't prove it."

"So we're OK then?" Biter asked hopefully.

"No, we're not OK. Far from it. I may not be able to have you arrested, but I do think I have a case for your dismissal," Dressel said with a smug look on his face.

"So you're going to fire me for one mistake? In all the years I've worked here, I've never had anything but a stellar evaluation."

"That's ancient history," Dressel replied. "You're a troublemaker. I'm actually happy you screwed up because now I have an excuse to get rid of you. Without you to agitate things, it should be a lot easier for me to gain the respect of the other keepers."

"Oh and how are you going to do that? By using me as an example and making them fear for their jobs? That's really a good way to motivate your employees."

"I don't need any lectures from you. I'm the one who's in charge, and I don't want anyone or anything to reflect negatively on this institution."

Biter became visibly angry and couldn't contain himself. "Who are you kidding? You don't care about the zoo. You never have. It's always been about the greater glory of James Dressel. We can't have a black mark on that pristine record of yours, now can we? Especially at this sensitive stage, when you're only the acting President," Biter said, purposely exaggerating the adjective.

"I'm sick of that stink eye look of yours. Who are you to judge me? This conversation is over. You're fired!" Dressel shrieked as he grabbed his radio and started to call security.

Biter wrested the radio out of his hand. "I don't need an escort out of here. You think I would do something to hurt the zoo? I love this place. It just shows how clueless you really are." He handed the handset back to Dressel, who was cowering in his chair. "I'm going to clean out my locker now. You can have security meet me there if you still feel I'm a threat. Have a nice life."

Wes was waiting apprehensively as Biter entered the keeper's room. "I heard Dressel's radio transmission."

"Yes," Biter said sadly. "I'm history. I'm going to miss you guys and all the animals."

Wes could see by the look on Biter's face that he was devastated by the thought of leaving the zoo. Wes wanted to do something to support his friend but was visibly conflicted. "I'd like to quit and walk out with you, but I have a family to support."

"No," Biter replied. "This is my deal, and I don't want anyone to go down with me."

Just then a security guard arrived to escort Biter off the premises. Biter looked at the man in disbelief. He was a friend of his, as well as a co-worker. The security guard lowered his head and said, "I'm sorry. I'm just doing my job."

Biter patted the man on his back. "No worries. I was just getting ready to leave." He turned to Wes and gave him a big hug.

"We'll still see each other, right?"

"I'm not going anywhere," Biter lied as he placed the last of his belongings from his locker into a paper bag and headed out the door.

THREE

Biter had made the six-hour trek from Eatonville, Washington to his best friend's house in Tidewater, Oregon countless times before, but today's trip seemed unusually long for some reason. He knew it was due, at least in part, to the anxiety and stress he felt because of his current financial situation. With little reserve funds, he was understandably worried about how he would be able to pay his bills. Not seeing any alternative, he had been forced to ask his best friend, JT, if he could stay at his place until he secured a new job. He knew that he and JT were as close as brothers and that he was always welcome in his friend's home. Still, he felt embarrassed, being in this situation, and was uncomfortable imposing on a friend like this.

As he traveled down the forested, one lane road that hugged the river's edge, Biter's spirits began to lighten. The sun had already dipped below the surrounding hills, and he knew the valley floor would soon be engulfed in shadows. He paused briefly to watch the barn swallows as they skirted back and forth, just inches above the water. He knew they were methodically working the river in an effort to catch their last share of insects before ceding the night sky to the bats, which would soon take wing.

The road he was traveling eventually diverged from the river and cut through a cow pasture, and he stopped to let a herd of wild elk, more than twenty strong, cross the road in front of him. He watched in awe as these large, hoofed mammals—some as large as 700 pounds or more—effortlessly scaled the four-foot fence that lined both sides of the road and bisected the pasture.

Although Biter had traveled this route countless times before, he realized for the first time that there was something special about this place. The Alsea River Valley was more than just the home of his best friend. It was also his personal sanctuary. He made the pilgrimage here as often as he could—on vacations, over the holidays and whenever the pressures of life, like now, proved to be too much for him to handle on his own.

Biter pulled into his friend's driveway and was relieved to see JT's maroon Ram 4x4 parked there. Eager to see his friend, he jumped out of his truck, ran up the steps to the front door and rang the doorbell. When there was no answer, he headed for the back of the house. Climbing up the steps to the deck that overlooked the river, he saw JT sprawled out in a deck chair, dressed in a Hawaiian shirt and shorts, sporting sunglasses and wearing a construction hard hat with a makeshift hummingbird feeder attached to the front of it.

So many birds were hovering around JT's head that it was difficult for Biter to see his friend's face. The pint-sized avians were so busy fighting for position in an effort to get access to the red nectar that they failed to notice his approach until he was nearly upon them. Upon discovering his presence, the hummingbirds flew off in all directions, conveying their indignation by emitting a rapid-fire series of high-pitched, nasal-sounding vocalizations.

Biter couldn't contain himself and began to laugh out loud. "What in blazes are you doing?"

"Hell, you're the biologist. You tell me," JT said teasingly. "It's called research, in case you've forgotten. I've watched the hummingbirds feed for years. I just thought it was time to get a closer look and a different perspective on what they do."

"Of course, I should have known," Biter said sarcastically. "What was I thinking?"

"Actually, I just got bored waiting for you to get here," JT confessed. "I was looking for something to keep me entertained until you arrived." JT was obviously pleased to see his friend. "Hey Cuz, you finally made it! You've had a long trip, and I bet you're a might thirsty right now. Go inside and get yourself a drink."

"That sounds like a plan," Biter said as he opened the sliding screen door and headed for the garage where he knew JT kept his keg cooler. "Can I get you anything?"

"Funny you should ask. I'll take a glass as well."

Upon entering the garage, Biter could see that JT had their favorite beer on tap, a barleywine. "Good choice," Biter yelled. As he filled two sixteen-ounce glasses, the image of JT in his hummingbird feeder/hard hat surfaced in his mind and warmed his heart. He found this image so appealing because it epitomized what he both respected and loved most about his friend. He knew JT was determined to enjoy himself each and every day of his life, no matter what. It didn't matter where he was or what the circumstances were. Biter knew JT would find a way to have fun. He found his friend's perspective on life refreshing and wished he could learn to approach his life in the same way. Returning to the deck, Biter once again made the hummingbirds scatter. He handed JT his pint of barleywine and sat down in a deck chair next to him.

JT took off his homemade, hummingbird feeder hat and placed it on the deck at the foot of his chair. Never one to dance around a subject, he asked pointedly, "Do we have to make small talk first or are you going to tell me why you stole the wolverine? You didn't give many details when we spoke on the phone, so I figured it must be a long story."

"I never said I stole the animal," Biter replied indignantly. "I said I returned it to the wild."

"Excuse me," JT countered, "but the animal belonged to the zoo, and you let it go. That's stealing in my book."

"It's a matter of perspective," Biter argued. "The animal was originally wild, and hence, not the property of anyone. It was caught by a trapper who sold it to the zoo. So it's not stealing. I just released the animal back from where it came, that's all."

JT laughed. "Give or take a thousand miles or so. Biter, you call it what you want, but it's still stealing. You don't have to get defensive. I'm not trying to judge you or your actions. I'm not even sure that I don't applaud what you did. I'm your best friend, and I'm just trying to understand why you did it."

Biter became defensive. "Maybe I don't know why."

JT took a drink and then stared contemplatively into the rusty brown liquid in his glass. "No, I think you do," he said honestly.

"The wolverine was frantically trying to escape," Biter offered. "I had a moment of weakness. The animal's desperation got to me, OK?"

"But you've seen this every time you've introduced a wild animal into an exhibit, and it's never had this effect on you before," JT argued. "What's the difference now?"

"It probably has something to do with my break up with Cassandra," Biter admitted grudgingly. "I guess I wasn't thinking straight."

"I think Cassandra's a sweetheart. The only negative thing I can say about her is that she obviously doesn't have good taste in men," JT said with a wink.

Biter raised his middle finger. "Very funny."

"Seriously, though. You guys seemed to be a good match, and I'm sorry that you broke up. Biter, I know you better than you know yourself, so bear with me here and let me hazard a guess. Cassandra was pressuring you to get married, and you hightailed it like a jackrabbit. Was that it?"

"Pretty much," Biter confessed. "I guess I value my freedom too much. I liked things the way they were. I made no demands on her. She was the one who was trying to change me."

A sad but knowing look came over JT's face. "Maybe her patience these past few years was her concession, and now it was time for you to make yours."

"Thank you, Mister Know-It-All," Biter replied with more than a hint of sarcasm.

"Biter, I love you like a brother, and I only want the best for you. It's your choice. I just think that, in this lifetime, you need to learn commitment." Seeing that his words were not being well received, JT changed the subject. "So tell me about the wolverine's release. Was it an emotional experience?"

"No, it was actually quite disappointing," Biter said sadly. "I guess, I was hoping for an interspecies, spiritual moment of some kind. Maybe some eye contact between me and the wolverine where I knew the animal appreciated the selfless act I had just committed on its behalf. Hell, I ended up losing my job because of it! But the animal just ran off without ever turning back."

JT was reluctant to say anything because he knew this would be a sensitive issue, but he felt compelled to tell Biter his true feelings. Looking him squarely in the eyes, he said, "Maybe it was because it wasn't a selfless act. You thought you were doing something good by giving the animal its life back, and you got the satisfaction of being in a position to make this happen. You felt good about yourself. Since you benefited from your action in some way, it wasn't a selfless act."

"So what about people who donate millions to charity? Are you telling me theirs aren't selfless acts?"

"First of all, the magnitude of the gift is not important," JT countered. "Is a gift of a million dollars from a rich individual more worthy than the more modest gift from someone like you or me, who might donate a hundred bucks to their favorite charity during the holiday season?"

"Duh...a million dollars, versus a hundred bucks? I think the answer's pretty damn clear."

JT started shaking his head before Biter had even finished. "No, it isn't clear at all. It depends on the person's capacity to give and his or her motivation. If you commit an act because it makes you feel good about yourself or because it will get you public recognition, then it isn't selfless. It may still be a generous act. It just isn't a selfless one."

"So you're saying that there's no such thing as a selfless act?"

"I don't know if there is such a thing. If there is, I think it is extremely rare. My inclination is to say, when you dissect an act down to its basic elements, you will always find there is some self-serving motivation there. I know you'll think I'm pulling your leg, but I can actually think of an act you committed, which comes as close to being a selfless act as anything I can come up with. Can you guess what it is?"

Biter looked at JT as if he was out of his mind. "Are you kidding me? You are giving me props? I wouldn't have a clue."

"This goes back a ways when we were both living in Tacoma. You may not even remember this story. It was when our friend Chris was renting a house on Proctor Street, near the University of Puget Sound. There was this senile old lady who lived next door to him. You were visiting Chris and met this woman out in front of his house when you were leaving one day. She was holding this scruffy, stuffed animal. I think it was a dog."

"Oh, now I remember," Biter said excitedly. "No, it was a cat. The plush animal was all matted down and dirty, but you could tell by the way she clung to it that she loved the thing. She told me she heard the cat calling to her one day and found it in a cupboard in her basement. She thought it was a real cat."

"And do you remember what else she said?"

"Yeah, I commented on the fact that 'kitty' looked like it needed a bath, and she said she agreed but didn't want to get soap in its eyes and make it cry."

JT knew the rest of the story, but he wanted to make Biter relive the moment so he asked him, "And then what happened?"

"I walked down to the mom-and-pop grocery that was at the end of the block and bought a small bottle of Johnson's Baby Shampoo and brought it back to her place and gave it to her. She started to tell me again that she didn't want to get soap in the cat's eyes and make it cry. I said I know. Look here on the bottle.

It says 'No more tears.' Oh, you would've thought I had given her a million bucks," Biter said as he broke into a laugh. "Her eyes lit up, and she was so happy!"

"Did you ever tell anybody about this incident before?"

"Hell, there was nothing to tell. The shampoo probably cost me less than three bucks. I had totally forgotten about this until you just brought it up. How do you even know about this anyway? I know I never told you."

"No. Chris did," JT replied. "It turns out the old lady was the mother of a Tacoma policeman who stopped Chris for speeding a few days after you gave his Mom the shampoo. The cop was getting ready to write Chris a ticket and noticed that the address on his license was the house next door to his Mom's place. The officer said that his mother had told him the story about the shampoo and the kindness you had shown her. He told Chris he figured anybody with a friend like that also had to be an upstanding guy, so he let him off with just a warning. Chris said it was because of you that he didn't get a ticket. I think it would have been a sizeable one too, like a couple of hundred bucks."

"How did Chris know it was me?"

"He didn't at first," JT answered. "He asked me if I had given the old lady the shampoo. That's how I found out about it. Chris said he couldn't think of anyone else who had come to his house around that time but you and me, so, by the process of elimination, we figured it had to be you."

"Hell, it seemed like nothing at the time. It still doesn't seem like much."

"Not to you, maybe, but it was obviously a big deal to that old lady. I'd say that's something. Yours was a simple act of kindness. You never mentioned your good deed to anyone, so it tells me you weren't motivated by self-aggrandizement. You obviously don't view it as a big deal even now, so I don't think you did it to feel good about yourself. I think you did it just because you felt at the time that it was the right thing to do. And that gave you some satisfaction, no matter how small. But the fact that you derived any satisfaction from the act at all, by definition, means that it was not a totally, selfless act. But it's as close to a selfless act that I can come up with."

Biter smiled broadly. "Thanks, JT. You made me feel good about myself. I've never been fired from a job before, and if the truth be known, I'm feeling kind of down right now. It's also mighty generous of you to let me stay here without paying any rent." Biter raised his glass in tribute to his friend. "So, thank you."

JT waved his hand in the air. "No thanks needed. I'm glad you're here. Don't get me wrong, I'm sorry you lost your job, but it provides us with the opportunity to spend more time together, and I'd be lying if I didn't admit I'm happy about that. Feel free to stay as long as you like."

Suddenly, the doorbell rang, and Biter sprang from his chair. "You stay put. I'll get the door." He slid the screen door open, walked through the living room and opened the front door. A man six feet, four inches in height, with a weathered face and a wiry, salt-and-pepper beard, stood in front of him. A crumpled black cowboy hat sat easily on the stranger's head, and he wore a faded and worn, blue plaid shirt, which was partially hidden by a black leather vest. He had a bloated stomach, which made him look pregnant, but Biter could tell from his muscular physique and his huge, calloused hands that the man was no stranger to hard work.

"Hello," the stranger said. "I hope I have the right house. JT does live here, doesn't he?"

"Are you a friend of his?"

"Yeah, I'm Ryan."

"Well come in. I'm JT's friend, Biter. He's out on the deck. Follow me."

Biter walked through the house to the deck with Ryan in tow. Opening the screen door, he said, "JT, a friend of yours is here."

JT looked up and saw the big cowboy. He jumped out of his chair. "Oh, shit. I forgot you were coming down! Hey cousin, it's good to see you." He turned to Biter. "This is my buddy, Ryan Moon." He then turned his attention back to the big cowboy. "Did you have any problems finding the place?"

"Yeah, a little. I lost your address but remembered you lived on Little Switzerland Road. I got down as far as the cattle ranch and didn't know which way to go when I got to the barn. So I asked a guy who was there unloading some hay for directions, but he wasn't any help."

JT collapsed back into his chair and grabbed his beer. "You know me. I like to keep a low profile. I don't give my name out to a lot of people."

"That's always wise," Ryan said as he lowered his large frame into an empty deck chair. "No worries. I didn't use your name. I said I'm looking for a friend whose house number adds up to twenty-two."

JT was in the midst of taking a drink when his mind registered the comment. He started laughing and coughing uncontrollably. "You asked him for a house number that adds up to twenty-two?"

"Yeah, I forgot the address, but I remembered that when you bought the house, you told me that the house number added up to twenty-two."

JT laughed so hard that tears started running down his face. "Right on. What did the rancher say?"

"He didn't say anything," Ryan responded. "He just gave me this confused look, so I headed down the road. I was looking for a place to turn around when I saw your truck in the driveway."

"Well, I'm sure you gave the rancher something to think about, and I'm glad you found the place, bro. That's awesome!"

Biter was also laughing so hard his stomach hurt. He knew right away that this guy was a stoner. He understood that anyone in his right mind would interpret Ryan's question as totally absurd, but he also knew it actually made perfect sense in a weird sort of way. It was common knowledge to all of JT's close friends that twenty-two was his favorite number. Biter had seen JT hit that number countless times when he was playing roulette in either Las Vegas or Reno.

The weird thing about it was that twenty-two seemed to be lucky for JT alone. When he, or another of JT's friends, would try to cash in on JT's luck by piggybacking on his number, twenty-two would never come in. JT noticed this as well and would get visibly annoyed when any of his friends would try to capitalize on his lucky number. It was as if he knew instinctively that it shut down his mojo with twenty-two and rendered his luck impotent. Biter knew this would sound crazy, but he also believed it to be true. More than once, he had witnessed JT winning on this number in consecutive spins of the wheel when he was playing it solo. He never saw JT win when he, or any of his other friends, had their money on it as well.

Smiling broadly, JT said, "Ryan, would you like some barleywine?"

"When have you known me to refuse?"

JT turned to Biter. "You know what we should do? We should fill up a container with beer and take Ryan up to see the migration. He'd love it."

Biter looked confused.

"You know," JT said. "You've seen it before. I'm talking about the newts."

Biter nodded. "Oh, now I know what you're talking about. I'll get the barleywine and meet you and Ryan at the truck."

Biter went into the kitchen and grabbed an empty half-gallon water jug and some plastic party cups and headed down to the garage to retrieve the beer. JT and Ryan headed out the door and got into Ryan's old beat-up, lime green GMC pickup. Biter placed the jug of barleywine and glasses in the bed of the truck, opened the passenger's door, and jumped in.

JT moved toward the middle of the seat, and Biter, as a joke, sidled up next to his friend, pretending he needed the extra room.

"Get off me Biter," JT said as he pushed back and compressed his friend against the passenger door. "Don't get too close to me. I don't want any of your DNA rubiture."

Ryan backed out of the driveway and headed up the road toward the highway. "So where are we going?"

"You'll see," JT replied. "We have to go a few miles upriver, and then we'll cross over a bridge and head up the ridge to a place that overlooks the house."

Once they crossed over the river, they headed up a dirt Forest Service road toward their destination. Later in the year, they would have left a trail of dust in their wake, but the relentless spring rains had only recently subsided, and the roadway was still moist and muddy. As they gained elevation, the river's sinuous path became more obvious. JT motioned for Ryan to head down a weed-covered offshoot, which dead-ended about a quarter mile off the main road.

When they couldn't drive any further, JT said, "We still have a ways to walk, but, it's not far."

As they proceeded down the overgrown road, its width narrowed steadily as the underbrush reclaimed more and more of the real estate Mother Nature had ceded to bulldozers years earlier. Red alders on opposing sides of the road competed for control of the canopy, but there was still enough sunlight penetrating the nest of branches to permit a fairly uniform, but not thick, growth of vegetation on the forest floor.

When they had gone about a quarter of a mile, JT led his friends to an opening on the river's side of the trail, which he had hacked out of the underbrush with a machete on an earlier trip to the site. The view looked like something one would see from a low flying plane. From their vantage point, they could see JT's house and his dock with two kayaks resting on it. They could also see that the ridge they were on blocked the river's forward progress and forced it to bend back on itself. JT's house was situated on the inside bend of the river.

As the trio of travelers continued down the path, they began to sense movement in the short grass in front of them. "Look! There's one," Biter said, as he pointed out a reddish-brown salamander about six inches long. Its limbs were splayed out to the sides in typical amphibian fashion as it slowly, but deliberately, lumbered across the trail in front of them.

JT asked incredulously, "One? Open your eyes, Biter. There are hundreds of them!"

As if on cue, Biter and Ryan expanded their focus and instantly saw what JT was seeing. The forest floor was alive with movement. Hundreds and hundreds of salamanders were moving in unison across the trail like a mud-colored army of diminutive soldiers with a common consciousness.

"Holy shit," Ryan said. "This is trippy! I've never seen so many salamanders in my life! What's going on?"

"They're rough-skinned newts," JT explained. "They're migrating to the river to breed."

"Yes, but what freaks me out," Biter added, "is why are they up at this elevation? We've got to be 300 or maybe 400 feet above the river. How did they get up here in the first place?"

"All I know is this is pretty cool," JT chuckled as he plopped himself down among the army of amphibians moving past him. He reached into his pocket and pulled out a pipe. "Biter, break out the barleywine."

Ryan and Biter sat down next to JT, being careful not to sit on any newts in the process. Biter poured the beer into plastic cups and passed them out to his companions. They toasted to the good time they were having. JT took a hit off the pipe and offered it to Biter.

Biter didn't smoke pot often, but this was a special occasion. He lived for times like this when he could immerse himself in nature and appreciate its intrinsic beauty. He could never understand why some people who considered themselves religious seemed to be threatened by science. In his experience, science didn't threaten his belief in God. It reinforced it. The more he learned about the natural world and how amazingly complex it was, the closer he felt to God and the firmer his belief in a higher being became.

Biter took a drag off the pipe, held it in his lungs as long as he could, and then started coughing violently as he passed the pipe to Ryan.

"That will get you stoned," JT said approvingly.

As the pot started to kick in, Biter sat silently, watching the seemingly endless wave of amphibians as they passed slowly by him and his friends. The newts showed no obvious signs of stress as they continued their journey at the same slow but steady pace. Biter was trying to decide whether they were just unconcerned or oblivious to their presence.

As he sat there contemplating this question, he noticed a newt, scaling a rock immediately in front of him. When the salamander reached the rock's summit, it lifted itself on its front limbs, arched its back and stared up at the sky. In this position, its bright, orange underside was clearly visible in the filtered sunlight. Biter thought this was probably some kind of defensive posture, but it was more fun to imagine something much more grandiose. "Hey, look at this one! He looks like he's doing yoga and contemplating the eternal."

"Yeah," JT said. "Or maybe you're just stoned."

Biter grabbed the newt off the rock and brought it close to his face, staring inquisitively into the yellow irises of its eyes. The shape of its mouth gave it a perpetual grin. It reminded Biter of the satisfied smirk someone might showcase if they knew a secret he didn't. He examined the animal's tiny, four-toed front feet and thought that, with the exception of the number of digits, they looked remarkably like the chubby little hands of a human fetus. Biter passed the newt to Ryan for a closer look.

"Maybe they're really aliens," Ryan offered. "They could be coming up here so the Mothership can pick them up and take them home."

Biter started laughing as he asked, "Where's home?"

"I don't know. I'm not an alien. Think about it. They're trippy looking. Aliens are trippy looking. Maybe we've been wrong in thinking they're a lot bigger than they are. Or maybe they can shrink themselves in preparation for space travel so their spaceships don't have to be that big. To get anywhere, they'd have to go at the speed of light, so smaller ships would be better."

Biter couldn't contain himself. "JT, you didn't tell me your buddy majored in physics," he said sarcastically.

"I wonder if this little fella's skin secretes a psychedelic substance like that of some frogs," Ryan said as he brought the newt up to his mouth and extended his tongue.

"No," Biter yelled as he grabbed the salamander out of Ryan's grasp. "Rough-skinned newts secrete a powerful neurotoxin! It would kill you! Biologists have found dead fish with these guys in their stomachs. The only animals that can eat them are garter snakes."

"No shit? How do you know all this?"

"Biter's a biologist," JT offered. "Or at least he was before the song "Born Free" got ingrained in his skull and made him crazy." JT gave Biter a wink to let him know it was all in good fun.

Biter didn't appreciate the reminder, but he knew JT didn't have a vindictive bone in his body. "Thanks, JT. That was special."

Ryan looked confused.

"I used to be a zookeeper," Biter explained, "but I got canned for letting a wolverine go."

"Awesome," Ryan said, obviously impressed. "What are you doing now?"

Biter and JT glanced at each other. "I'm kind of in between jobs at the moment," Biter confessed.

"I'm sorry to hear that," Ryan said with genuine remorse. "I'm taking a couple of city folk up into the woods on a horsepack trip a week from now and could use a trailhand. Would you be interested? It doesn't pay a lot, but you'd see some pretty country and get to do some fishing."

"I'm not sure. I can ride a horse, but I don't know the first thing about being a trailhand. I'd probably be more of a hindrance than a help."

"That's OK. I'd just like to have some company. The guys I'm taking are businessmen from Seattle who fancy themselves as environmentalists. I don't want to have to wet nurse those yahoos. That would be your main job. Plus, I know they would really get off on your scientific mumbo jumbo."

"You should do it, Biter," JT added. "You'll go crazy without a job, and it would be good for your mental state."

Biter knew JT was right. "Thanks for the vote of confidence, Ryan. I'm your man."

FOUR

As Biter drove slowly down the long, pothole-ridden driveway leading to Ryan's mobile home, he got his first glimpse of the horses that would carry him and his fellow travelers on their twenty-mile trip into the Pasayten Wilderness. He was struck by how different the animals appeared.

Two were fairly large, maybe fifteen hands at the shoulder, and looked to Biter like they were in their prime, but Biter had little experience with horses. He had spent the first eighteen years of his life in New Jersey and had ridden horses only at a Boy Scout Camp when he was maybe ten or eleven. He had, however, worked around hoofed animals long enough in the zoo to recognize an ungulate's relative age and vigor.

Two of the other horses were obviously in good health but gave Biter the impression they had more than a few miles on them. He thought of a line he especially liked from the first Indiana Jones movie. Indy had said to his female love interest, "It's not the years. It's the mileage." Biter couldn't count the number of times he felt this line applied to him, but he sensed it was equally appropriate here.

The remaining horse was smaller than the others and had some characteristics you would normally associate with a pony. It had a thick mane and was big-boned. It also appeared to be the oldest and was by far the most muscular of the lot. This, coupled with its compact frame, gave the horse an appearance of power not equaled by his larger brethren.

Biter wondered what criteria Ryan would use to pair up the horses with their riders. Physical size would obviously be an important consideration, but the horse's temperament and the rider's relative experience would also be factors to consider.

As Biter reached the end of the driveway, Ryan opened up the screen door and waited for his guest to exit his vehicle. "Biter, what took you so long? I thought you'd be here an hour ago."

"Yeah, I know," Biter answered. "I got a late start."

"Well, come on in. Dinner's nearly ready. I hope you like trout."

As Ryan turned his attention to the skillet on the stove, he said, "Get yourself a beer out of the ice chest near the refrigerator."

Biter was ready for a beer. The trip to Ryan's house was a ten-hour drive, and he was sore from sitting in one position for so long. As he grabbed a cold one out of the cooler, he walked into the living room. He could still see Ryan from his vantage point because the living area was only separated from the kitchen by a cooking island.

Biter believed that, by looking around a person's home, he could get a sense of what was important in that person's life. As he scanned the room, he noticed that there were framed pictures of horses and cowboys on the walls. There was also a pair of old rusty spurs and a shadow box with different types of barbed wire displayed on an end table. A coffee table held a half-filled bowl of stale popcorn and a framed photo of Ryan and a child Biter guessed was Ryan's son. Biter picked up the photo to get a better look at the grinning, little tyke in the picture. "Is this your son? He's a cute kid."

"Yeah, that's Luke," Ryan said. "He was six when that picture was taken. My wife Lisa took him back East to live with her folks when we split up. I haven't seen him in a couple of years. It's not that I don't want to. She just won't let me. Her folks have money and can afford better lawyers. It sucks."

Biter put the picture back on the coffee table, downed the rest of his beer and took another out of the cooler before joining Ryan in the kitchen area.

"So, have you lived in this area all your life?"

"No," Ryan answered. "I was born and raised in Seattle. My Dad was a professor at the University of Washington in the School of Engineering. I moved here after my Dad died. I've been here about fifteen years."

"Did you go to the 'UW' too?"

"No, I was never any good in school. I'm dyslexic. My teachers used to think I was stupid, and then they found a name for it. I worked as a tradesman for years before my Dad passed away. He left me a small inheritance so I don't need to work if I don't want to, but I still do odd jobs now and again."

Ryan took a pot of rice off the stove and placed it on a hot pad on the kitchen table. A bowl of mixed vegetables, a stick of margarine on a saucer, a bag of stale dinner rolls and an assortment of condiments were already laid out on the table.

Ryan motioned for Biter to take a seat at the table as he removed a large trout from the frying pan and placed it on Biter's plate. He put another fish of roughly equal size on his plate, returned the skillet to the stove and sat down across the table from Biter.

"Dig in," Ryan said.

Biter was hungry from his long drive and loaded healthy portions of rice and veggies on his plate. He grabbed his fork, dissected a large section of the trout, and eagerly placed it in his mouth. At the first taste of the fish, he lost his appetite. The fish looked pleasing enough, but it had a funny aroma and an even more unusual taste. He quickly swallowed the food to get the unpleasant taste out of his mouth.

Biter didn't want to offend his host, so he resorted to a tactic he had learned as a kid. When confronted with food he found unpalatable, he smothered the offending item in ketchup and cut off small parcels and then buried them in much larger helpings of some other food he deemed acceptable. Using this technique, he knew it would take him some time to consume the weird tasting trout, and he would be forced to eat even more rice and vegetables than he cared to.

Biter grabbed the ketchup bottle and unloaded a quarter of its contents on his plate. He did the same with the tartar sauce. He then grabbed several dinner rolls out of the previously untouched bag and loaded them with big slabs of margarine.

He then began the long process of consuming the food that was on his plate. He cut off an inch-long section of fish, drowned it in a puddle of ketchup and placed it in his mouth, followed shortly thereafter by a huge helping of rice.

"So Ryan, I saw the horses when I drove up. Are we taking all of them on our trip?"

"Yeah, we've got four people, so we'll ride four and use Tiny as the pack animal."

"I'm assuming Tiny is the smallest one. He looks like he'd be a good pack animal."

"He's small, but he's mighty. He's getting old though, and I don't know how many more years he can go on these trips."

Biter consumed another forkful of fish, this time covered in tartar sauce. He followed it with a margarine-coated dinner roll and took a big gulp of beer to wash it down. "What are the names of the other horses?"

"Well, there's Tiny. And the others are named Bert, Ernie, Bilbo, and Gandalf."

Biter thought the choice of names was unusual. "Did you name your horses yourself?"

"No," Ryan responded. "My son named my horses."

Biter looked confused. "So your six-year-old son was into *Sesame Street* and Tolkien's *The Hobbit?*"

"I don't know what Toolkit's *The Hobbit* is. But, yeah, my son liked *Sesame Street*."

Biter swallowed another smothered concoction of fish and veggies. "But you said your son named your horses. Bilbo and Gandalf are obviously characters from the book, *The Hobbit.*"

"Like I said, I don't know what *The Hobbit* is. My son named my horses. Bert and Ernie are my horses. So is Tiny, but I've had him for years, long before my son was born. Bilbo and Gandalf belong to my neighbor. I'm just borrowing them for this trip."

Biter started to laugh. He was beginning to understand how Ryan's mind worked and how he would have to communicate with him if this trip was going to work.

Ryan took a swig of beer and asked, "So did you get the steaks and other provisions I asked you to pick up at the store?"

"Yep," Biter responded as he ate another forkful of his meal. "They're in the cooler in the bed of my truck. I also got a case of beer and a bottle of Jack Daniels for our trip."

"The Jack's fine," Ryan said. "But you can't take the beer. It's too much weight for the horse you'll be riding."

"Which horse will I be riding?"

"Bert. He's the one I normally ride. I know you haven't had a lot of experience on horses, and he'll be no problem."

"Ryan, what do you weigh? 250? 275? I weigh a buck fifty. Even with the beer, Bert will be carrying a lot less weight than when you're riding him."

"Yeah," Ryan responded. "But it's dead weight. No way. You're not taking it."

Biter looked down and removed the remaining fish from his plate. A sly smirk crossed his face. He said nothing but made a mental note, make sure you hide the beer.

As Biter swallowed his last forkful of fish, Ryan said, "There's more trout in the skillet if you're still hungry."

Biter pretended to be full. "No, thanks, I'm stuffed."

"Yeah," Ryan said. "It tasted like shit. My freezer went out about a week ago. I probably should have thrown the fish out."

Biter was incredulous but said nothing. He immediately grabbed another beer from the cooler and pounded it. He then went out to his car to retrieve his sleeping bag. When he returned, he asked Ryan where he would be sleeping.

Ryan showed him to his son's room. Biter turned on the light and saw that the bed was covered by a thick layer of dust and that there were dead houseflies strewn across the bedspread.

"I probably should have vacuumed the place before you got here," Ryan offered. "But I hate cleaning."

"That's OK," Biter said with a nervous laugh as he laid his sleeping bag on the bed. "This is a camping trip, right? I'll see you in the morning."

FIVE

Ryan had been leading his caravan of neophytes on their trek into the Pasayten Wilderness for three hours, and his charges, though initially a little uneasy, had become comfortable with their mounts and were now beginning to enjoy the scenery. The team had been steadily gaining elevation, but the climb had been gradual, and the fact that they had been in the thick of the forest made it even more difficult to gauge just how high they had climbed. Ryan had wisely sandwiched his paying customers, the two Seattle businessmen, in between himself and Biter. Ryan led the string, and Biter took up the rear leading Tiny, who served as the pack animal.

As the foursome crossed a talus slope, Biter heard the familiar high-pitched whistle of a marmot. He had frequently encountered these animals in earlier hiking trips in both the Cascades and Olympic Mountains in Washington. The presence of these alpine residents made him realize just how high they had climbed since they had embarked from the trailhead.

His eyes scanned the rocky slope, hoping to catch a glimpse of its inhabitants. There were several marmots, peeking out of their burrows as the team of horses passed by. Biter recognized immediately the species from the white patches on their muzzles and the silver-grey fur on their shoulders and upper backs. "Hey guys, look at the hoary marmots," Biter said, eager to establish his role as the team's resident naturalist. "Did you hear that high-pitched whistle just before we got to the rocks? It's their alarm call. It's how they warn the others in their group of impending danger. In fact, it's because of this call that they're nicknamed whistle pigs. They're the largest ground squirrels in North America."

"The marmots aren't really that afraid of us," Ryan added. "You should see how they act when they really feel threatened. I saw a golden eagle once swoop down and grab one of these little fellas in its six-inch tongs. The others went apeshit and made a beeline for their holes. You didn't see any of them peeking out of their dens like they're doin' now."

Larry, a tall, lean software executive, and his friend and co-worker Ethan started laughing hysterically. "The eagle was probably in the middle of making a salad when he saw the marmot," Larry joked. Biter knew they were laughing at Ryan's malapropism, but he couldn't help himself and joined in. At first he felt guilty enjoying a laugh at his new friend's expense, but then Ryan started laughing, and it seemed harmless enough. He knew Ryan had no clue what everyone thought was so funny and guessed he joined in just because he wanted to enjoy the moment.

As the distance between the riders and the marmots widened, Ethan looked back, saw the marmots resuming their favorite sunning spots on the boulders and said, "Those fat, little bastards have the life. They're adorable." Biter was amused at Ethan's response. It was the same way many people react to squirrels in a city park. Because they're cute, people like them. How different, he thought, was the average person's reaction to a mouse or a rat? They're rodents as well, but they have the misfortune of not possessing the cute factor.

Biter likened this to the advantage an attractive person has over someone short on looks in a job interview. Most people assume a good-looking person will be charming and intelligent. While this may be a misconception, which is dispelled the first time the person opens his or her mouth, an average-looking person enjoys no such positive presumption of net worth. He had to admit that he himself harbored this superficial prejudice in his youth, when he was more susceptible to peer pressure and the power of advertising. As he got older, looks became less important to him, and he felt he had become a better judge of character.

As they left the rockslide, the trail narrowed steadily until it was barely wider than the width of the horses. The ridge they were hugging rose high above their heads on their left, and there was a fairly steep but not precipitous drop off into the canyon on their right.

Ryan was very familiar with the route they were traveling and understandably registered no uneasiness with the narrowness of the trail. More surprising, however, was the lack of concern evidenced by his fellow travelers. They seemed confident in their horses' abilities to navigate the narrow trail and showed no signs of anxiety. The Seattle contingent listened to their Walkmans while Biter enjoyed the view and sipped from the flask of Jack Daniels he had retrieved from his saddlebags.

Ryan took a can of Copenhagen out of his shirt pocket, put a dip in his lower lip and fed a little to his horse. As he placed the can back in his pocket, his horse Ernie stepped into an abandoned mouse burrow, which was now occupied by a colony of yellow jackets. Within seconds, the yellow and black, winged terrors were swarming out of their nest and indiscriminately attacking horses and riders alike.

Ryan's horse Ernie was the first to be stung, setting off a chain reaction as he started to buck. The other horses, following close behind, backed up abruptly and began to kick wildly as their riders waved their arms and hats in a futile attempt to fend off the angry insects. Everyone was yelling at the top of their lungs as they hung on to their saddle horns with death grips, trying not to be jettisoned from their mounts.

Two yellow jackets landed on Biter's face, stinging him on his nose and lips. As he swatted at his face to remove his winged attackers, his horse Bert lunged backwards, forcing the pack horse Tiny to step off the trail. As the horse struggled to regain his footing, Biter instinctively grabbed Tiny's reins, which were loosely wrapped around his saddle horn, and released them. He watched in horror as the animal rolled down the slope to the valley floor. With each full roll over, more and more of the gear that was lashed to the pack frame on Tiny's back broke free—cooking utensils, canned food, clothing, camping tents and the cans of beer Biter had hidden in a sleeping bag, cascaded down the slope, fanning out in all directions.

Ryan instinctively dug his spurs into his horse's flanks in an effort to escape the wrath of the insects. As his horse raced forward, the others followed in close pursuit. When the yellow jackets ceased to be a threat, Ryan dismounted and ran back to Biter, who was also getting off his horse. "You guys stay here with the horses," Ryan said to Larry and Ethan. "Biter and I will go down to check on Tiny."

Once he was out of earshot of his charges, Ryan whispered, "Jeezus, Biter, I've never had this happen before. These city guys are going to start freaking out. You know how I know?"

Biter shook his head in the negative.

"Because I'm freaking out. I just told you I've never had this happen before! I don't know what I'm going to do if I need to put Tiny down. I'm afraid I'll lose it! He and I go back a long way. I love that animal."

All Biter could say was, "I know." The two of them then started to climb down the ridge as fast as the steepness of the slope would allow. Ryan's focus was on getting to Tiny as quickly as he could. Biter wisely understood his job was to collect as much of the discarded gear as possible and to move it incrementally down to the valley floor.

As Biter continued to move his ever-enlarging pile of supplies down the slope, he repeatedly checked out the status of the situation that was unfolding below. He saw that Ryan had finally made it to the valley floor and was assessing the extent of Tiny's injuries. The horse was now on his feet, and Ryan was lifting each of the animal's legs and looking for any signs of fractures. He then ran his hands along the horse's back and undersides as he checked closely for any signs of gashes or puncture wounds.

When Biter had finally dragged as much of the gear as he could to the valley floor, he ran over to Ryan to get his assessment of the horse's injuries.

"Biter, your nose and lips are all puffed up! You look like you've been in a fight. I hope you don't have an allergic reaction to bee stings cause I'm not going to do any mouth-to-mouth regurgitation."

"Never mind me," Biter said. "How's Tiny?"

"Either it's a miracle or Tiny is one tough son of a bitch," Ryan said with a sigh of relief. "I've checked every inch of the animal, and he seems to be OK. Sure, he's beat up a little, but there's no broken bones. I can't believe it!"

"That's great news," Biter exclaimed. "How do we get Tiny back up the hill?"

"Are you kidding me? There's no way we could get a healthy horse up that slope. You're going to have to walk Tiny out of the canyon and hook up with us further down the trail. Leave the canned goods and the beer." Ryan suddenly became visibly angry. "I told you not to bring that beer. I told you it was too heavy!"

"The beer didn't cause this. The yellow jackets did," Biter argued.

"The beer stays here. Just take the perishables, cooking utensils and clothing and leave the canned goods. We'll catch trout and shoot some fool hens. We won't starve."

"But I don't know where we are going," Biter protested.

"You'll be fine," Ryan said. "Here's a compass. If you just go north for about another ten miles or so, you'll pretty much run into the place where we'll be camped. You might be a little off, but I think you should be able to see the lake we'll be at."

"Ryan, I have a bad feeling about this. I didn't tell you, but I've had a bad experience in the woods before. I don't think I can do this."

"Sorry Biter, you got a better idea? I've got to get back to the guys that are paying for this trip before they start freaking out. You should be fine as long as you get there before dark."

"Thanks, Ryan. That's reassuring." Biter grabbed a can of beer from the pile of gear he brought down the ridge and sat down dejectedly on a nurse log. As he cracked it open and raised the can to his swollen lips, the frothy liquid flowed over his fingers. He sipped the suds and watched Ryan's progress as he slowly climbed the slope and rejoined the rest of the riding party.

"See you at camp," Ryan yelled as the team of riders resumed their journey and disappeared from sight. Biter finished his beer, retrieved another and walked over to Tiny. He stretched out his free hand and rubbed the horse's neck. As he gently ran his hand over the animal, he asked, "Are we having fun yet?"

It took nearly an hour for Biter to sort through the gear, repack the essentials and secure them on the pack frame. He hated the thought of wasting beer so he drank while he worked, consuming another four in the process. When he was ready to embark, he took off his T-shirt, stuffed six cans of beer inside the shirt and tied it to a stick in hobo fashion. He opened one last beer for the road, placed his hobo suitcase over his shoulder, grabbed Tiny's reins and headed north.

After several miles, he encountered a heavily traveled game trail, which seemed to head in the direction he and Tiny were traveling. Since he knew that animals were adept at finding the most efficient routes through rough terrain, he followed the trail but checked his compass periodically to ensure he was maintaining a northward course. An hour later, the game trail intersected with what appeared to be a major hiking trail. Biter became elated as he gained confidence that he might, indeed, once again meet up with his fellow travelers.

Unfortunately, his heightened spirits lasted for less than three miles. The trail broke off into two branches, and Biter was frozen with indecision. He felt his blood pressure elevate and his heart rate quicken. He cursed Ryan for putting him in this situation. He took a series of deep breaths in an attempt to keep from having a panic attack. He looked at Tiny, who evidenced no such discomfort. He knew that the animal had no clue what was freaking him out, but he envied the animal's lack of concern nonetheless. There was something refreshing about Tiny's stoicism.

Biter inspected both segments of the trail in the hope that one leg would appear to be more heavily traveled than the other. The substrate, however, was mostly shale, and what soil existed was about equally pockmarked with hoof and human footprints. Biter retrieved a beer from his T-shirt on a stick and sat down on a rock to consider his alternatives.

Suddenly, a Great Gray Owl left its perch in a larch tree and flew toward him. Biter looked skyward as the large raptor flew silently overhead. He followed the bird's progress as it continued on its way through the forest canopy. He cherished moments like this when he had the opportunity to observe seldom-seen animals in their natural habitats. He regarded the rarity of the experience as a special gift and knew that his memory of this day years later would be as vivid in his mind as it was now. As he sat there savoring the moment, he placed his beer on the ground and noticed that there was a barred feather in the trail immediately in front of him. He recognized it as a primary feather from an owl by its serrated, leading edge and knew that this was in part what gave these birds the ability of silent flight. But was this feather from the Great Gray Owl he had just witnessed or had it been lying there all along?

The end of the feather's vane was pointing in the direction of the right hand fork of the trail. Was this an omen? Biter wanted to believe it was but needed more proof to convince him. He picked up the feather, raised it above his head and released it, letting it fall slowly to the ground. This time the feather's vane pointed to the left fork of the trail. Biter was angry with himself for seeking validation that the feather was indeed an omen. Had he accepted the feather's original position as a sign, he would have been on his way, albeit with a false sense of confidence. In this case, blind faith would have been better than the indecision he still faced.

As the sun continued to wane, he knew he had to make a decision. He had been traveling for hours and assumed he must be close to the lake. He grabbed his Ruger .44 from his shoulder holster and fired it in the air three times. He hoped Ryan would hear the shots and fire back, revealing the direction in which he should travel.

He listened intently for a response. There was only silence. He withdrew his handgun once again and fired off three more volleys. Again his shots were left unanswered.

"Screw it," Biter said disgustedly. He grabbed Tiny's reins and headed up the right fork of the trail. As he gained elevation, he moved ever faster in an effort to reach the crest of the ridge before the last rays of the sun disappeared behind the surrounding hills. When he reached the summit, he got his first glimpse of the glacier-carved lake below. Half of the lake was still frozen, and the moonshine, reflecting off the ice, contrasted sharply with the obsidian black of the lake's unfrozen end, giving the body of water the appearance of a giant black-and-white cookie. To his relief, there was a campfire on the eastern shore of the lake, and he could discern the black stick figures of humans huddled around it.

He took a flashlight out of a saddlebag and hurried down the trail. In less than an hour, he was at the camp. As he approached the fire, he saw Ryan, anxiously awaiting his arrival. His friend's face was illuminated by the flames. "Shit, Biter, it took you long enough to get here." He offered Biter a flask of whiskey as a welcome. "I was starting to get worried. Tiny's carrying most of the food, and we're getting hungry."

Biter grabbed the flask and took a healthy swig. "Tiny and I are both fine. Thanks for asking," Biter said sarcastically as he handed the flask back to Ryan. "Did you, by any chance, hear three gun shots? And then three more shortly after that?"

"Yeah, it sounded like a distress signal."

For a second, the stupidity of Ryan's answer rendered Biter speechless. Just as he was about to vent his anger, Larry and Ethan started laughing. Biter wanted to be angry, but he was so relieved to be reunited with his party that he broke into laughter as well. "That's what I like about you, Ryan. You're always thinking."

Biter walked over to Tiny and started removing the gear from the pack frame. He gave the cooler with the perishables to Ryan and said, "I figured we'd have steaks the first night of our trip. I forget where I packed the metal grill to cook them on. It will take me a couple of minutes to find it."

"Don't bother," Ryan said. "We'll just throw them in the fire and cook them Indian style." He started to unwrap the meat, and Biter quickly grabbed the package out of his hands.

"I don't think the Indians had Porterhouse," Biter countered. "You just relax. I'll do the cooking."

"You're alright, Biter. I don't care what anybody else says about you," Ryan chuckled as he returned to his seat on a log next to Larry and Ethan. "Tonight's meal is being prepared by Chef Biter."

"We've certainly had an exciting day," Larry said as he took a hit off a joint and passed it to Ryan. "Are all of your trips this eventful?"

"No, Tiny doesn't usually fall off the trail."

"On our way here, you told us this was Biter's first trip with you. Did you have a trailhand on your earlier trips or did you do it all yourself?"

Ryan took a drag off the joint and passed it to Ethan. "This is the first trip in five years my friend Jay hasn't come along. We kind of had a falling out. After the last trip, he told me he was tired of my bullshit and didn't want to go any more."

"That's harsh," Ethan offered. "What happened to cause the riff?"

"Nothing I could figure. He just started acting weird when he turned fifty. I just thought he was going through a midwife crisis."

Ethan started laughing so hard that tears started streaming down his face. Larry was also in stitches. Biter just shook his head with a big grin on his face as he stuck a fork in one of the steaks to see if it was done. A growing cloud of blue-gray smoke from the grill hung over their heads like a community halo. All in all it was a good day, Biter thought.

SIX

JT was ensconced in an armchair in his living room, watching the day's NASCAR race on his TV when the doorbell rang. Not wanting to miss any of the action, he considered not answering the door, but his unknown visitor depressed the doorbell again within seconds of the first ring. Sensing that this person was both impatient and persistent, he grudgingly got out of his chair and headed for the door. OK, this better be good, he thought to himself.

Opening the door, he saw Biter standing in front of him. His hair was greasy and matted down, and he obviously hadn't shaved in a week. While this was expected, his face was also covered in a multitude of scabs.

"Hello, spleen merchant," JT said with an obvious smile on his face. "You're back early. Did you lose your keys?"

"They're somewhere in my pack, but I didn't want to have to deal with looking for them right now," Biter said with obvious irritation in his voice.

"Were you attacked by mosquitoes? I can't help but notice the scabs all over your face. I didn't think it was possible, but you actually look worse than you normally do."

"Thanks for the compliment. No, it was deer flies," Biter countered. "I can't tell you how much fun it was going on a pack trip with your friend."

JT chuckled. "I thought you liked Ryan?"

"It's a long story."

"Well, calm down, get a beer from the garage, and come back upstairs. Get me one too. I want to hear all about it," JT said as he headed back to his chair.

Biter unloaded his gear in the entryway and went to the garage to retrieve the barleywine.

Returning to the living room, Biter handed JT his beer and plopped down in the padded wing chair next to him. JT turned the sound down on his television, took a swig of his barleywine and said, "So what happened?"

Biter unloaded on JT with a litany of grievances. "The whole trip was a comedy of errors. We got attacked by yellow jackets, our packhorse fell off the trail and our party got split up. Ryan led the paying customers to the lake, and he left me with Tiny at the bottom of the canyon to find our own way to camp. After a ten-mile trip on foot, I finally found my way to the lake and reconnected with Ryan and the others. The next day the temperature warmed up, and the deer flies made their presence known with a vengeance. I've never seen such god-awful insects in my life. You try to brush them off you, and they don't even move. You should've seen the horses. They were bleeding all over. I've never seen anything like it."

JT couldn't help himself and laughed heartily. "And of course, you had to scratch the hell out of your bites until you removed all of your skin."

"The itching was driving me crazy," Biter said defensively.

"Biter, you do the same thing every time you have a pain somewhere. You rub the hell out of the area and make it worse."

"I don't start rubbing a spot until it hurts. It doesn't start hurting because I was rubbing it for no reason."

"No, but by rubbing it, you make it worse," JT countered. "I think we need to duct tape oven mitts over your hands so you can't scratch off the scabs on your face until they have a chance to heal."

"I thought you wanted to hear about the trip?"

"Well, I think you've already given me the high points, or should I say—from your perspective—the low points of the trip. If I heard you correctly, one of Ryan's horses fell off the trail, and you had to find your own way to the lake. Anyone would find that experience harrowing, but in your case, I think it would be especially stressful. Did it bring back bad memories of when you were lost on Mt. Adams?"

"I'd be lying if I said it didn't."

JT's face suddenly turned gray and serious. "I still remember that trip as if it was yesterday. Everyone thought you were dead, and, by all rights, you should have been after what you went through. It was no picnic for us either. Heller and I went through hell that night as well, waiting in vain for you to return." Tears welled up in JT's eyes. "I'll never forget the moment we found out you were still alive. It was incredible!"

Biter extended his hand, and JT covered it with both of his. Looking directly in Biter's eyes, JT said, "I know it will sound crazy, but I think that experience was meant to cement our friendship."

The two friends then spent the next hour sipping their beers and reliving the moments of that seminal experience.

SEVEN

Shivering violently, Biter arrived at the false summit on Mt. Adams, a mountain in southwestern Washington State, wearing nothing more than a perspiration-soaked T-shirt and cotton jeans. An hour earlier, JT and their mutual friend, Tim Heller, had gotten tired of his slow pace and had forged ahead, leaving him a good quarter mile behind. From his vantage point, Biter could now see his friends making their final ascent to the top of the mountain. He wanted desperately to join them but was tired, wet and cold and had no warm clothes to protect him. He reluctantly decided to abandon his climb and retreated slightly from the false crest to gain some respite from the brunt of the unrelenting wind. He sat down in the snow to rest while he waited for his friends to return and watched a train of jet-black storm clouds as they advanced from the west. Eventually, the combined effect of his evaporating perspiration and the relentless assault of the wind got the best of him, and he glissaded down the mountain to a traditional rendezvous spot called "Lunch Counter." He took off his pack, used it as a seat and waited patiently for his friends to return.

Biter was angry with himself for his stupidity. Yes, he thought, today's outing was intended to be a day hike, and the weather had been forecast to be beautiful. But he had climbed Mt. Rainier and several other large peaks in the Cascades and Olympics before this and knew better than to go into the mountains at any time of the year without the proper gear. In fact, he usually packed much more gear than what was needed and ended up coming home with at least a week's worth of food.

Their plan was to hike to the top of the mountain and ski, snowboard or hike down. His first mistake was choosing downhill skis as his method of descent. He had underestimated the weight and bulkiness of the equipment. His second mistake was relying on the promise of good weather and jettisoning the warm clothes he had intended to pack in favor of a lighter load. His third mistake was drinking too much the night before the climb.

Earlier that morning, he had started the climb with a king-sized headache. He had tried all of his traditional home remedies to lessen the pain, but nothing seemed to work. Not the six aspirin he had chased with a quart of water, not the high carb trail mix he had forced himself to consume, and not the two hair-of-the-dog beers he had pounded as a last resort.

Thankfully, his hangover had run its course, and he was now feeling human again. He sat on the snow and waited for his friends to return. He looked downhill and could see a series of rock outcroppings, jutting out of the snow. He knew he had stashed his skis, poles, and boots in one of these rock islands on the way up the mountain, but he now realized he couldn't remember which one held his gear.

Before this realization could play with his confidence, Tim Heller surprised him and broke his concentration. "Biter, you're getting old. I can't believe you didn't join us at the top."

"I could have made it if I brought the proper gear," Biter said defensively. "But I felt shitty all day and was cold. I don't have anything to prove."

"Oh, don't be so defensive. I'm just giving you shit."

"Do you have any beer left?"

Heller opened his pack and took out three beers. "I'm not an alcoholic like you. I know how to pace myself."

"I'm happy for you. Now can I have a beer?"

"Biter, you're always so angry," Heller chuckled. "Here you go."

JT also grabbed a beer from Heller and said, "OK, girls don't fight. Seriously, Biter, I wish you would have joined us at the summit."

"I wanted to," Biter said before JT cut him off.

"I just wanted you to be there with us, brother. Your clothes are all wet, and you look real cold. Let's just finish these beers and head down."

"No argument there," Biter replied.

The trio chugged their beers and headed down the mountain. When they got to the first rock outcropping, JT and Heller waited for Biter as he searched the cavities around the rocks for his skis. When he came up empty-handed, JT jumped up on his snowboard and said, "I'll see you guys back at camp." As he headed down the slope, Biter and Heller hiked down to the next island of rocks in the snow. When Biter once again failed to find his skis, Heller said, "I'm heading down too. When I get to the next series of rocks, I'll check to see if your skis are there. If they are, I'll wave so you know I found them. If I don't signal, it means you can skip these and head down to the next ones."

Heller proceeded down at a more rapid pace than Biter, and the slope was such that he soon disappeared from sight. When Biter made it to the next set of rocks, Heller was nowhere to be seen. Biter searched in the cavities around the boulders and finally located his gear. Relieved, he put on his skis, donned his Walkman and headed down the mountain to the accompaniment of Soundgarden's "Black Hole Sun."

After the drudgery of the hike, the effortlessness of the descent was intoxicating, and he gave himself up completely to the moment, enjoying the scenery and the music, as he carved his way down the slope. When he got to the tree line, the snow began to peter out, and he was forced to pay more attention to the path he was taking. He continued on the snow as long as he could, circumventing rocks and bare patches of dirt, to remain on his skis as long as possible. When he came to the end of the snow, he removed his skis, put on his hiking boots, secured his gear to his backpack, and continued his descent. As he made his way down, he had every confidence that he would find the trail that would take him back to his campsite. His heart sank as he came to the edge of a ravine and saw a river at the base of the chasm. He was lost!

EIGHT

Biter had not encountered a river on the ascent. In the morning, he let Heller lead the way and had not paid attention on the way up. Consequently, he had no markers to tell him he was on the right path. He turned and immediately began to retrace his steps, hoping that he would be able to locate Heller's tracks and follow them back to camp. When he reached the edge of the trees, he could see the storm clouds advancing and realized it would be dark before he could make it to the spot where he and Heller had separated. He knew he wouldn't be able to find his way in the dark without a flashlight and that there was no way in hell he'd be able to survive the biting cold that threatened to overtake him if he remained in the open. He decided he had no choice but to retreat back down the slope and attempt to find a protected place in the trees where he could weather the storm and somehow make it through the night.

When he was no longer in the snow, he began his search for a suitable place to spend the night. He settled on a spot below a large fir tree and was about to remove his pack when he heard a high-pitched scream. His heart sank as his mind recognized the source of the sound. He looked skyward, nervously seeking to confirm what his brain already knew. He saw the unmistakable silhouette of a big cat perched on a tree limb about twenty feet above his head. It was a cougar!

As it stared menacingly down on Biter, the big cat emitted a low-pitched hiss. All Biter could focus on were the animal's piercing, yellow eyes and its inch-and-a-half long canines. To Biter, it looked like a demonic Cheshire cat. He wanted to run like hell, but he knew if he moved too quickly, it might provoke an attack. He hoped that the pack on his back made him appear bigger than he really was and that this would deter the cat from attacking him.

With his heart pounding wildly in his chest, he slowly backed away from the big cat. He didn't turn his back on the animal until he was at least a good fifty feet from its location. Even then, it took all of his reserves to maintain a slow retreat. He didn't pick up his pace until he was at least a hundred yards away.

When he had traveled about a quarter mile, he began to relax and once again started looking for a protected place to spend the night. A thick fog was settling in, making it difficult to see. Biter found another large fir that he thought offered some protection from the prevailing wind and settled on this as the place where he would spend the night. Before he removed his pack, he looked above his head to be sure there was nothing lurking in the branches that might want to make him its next meal. The fog was so thick, he couldn't really see anything but the lowest branches, but this gave him some solace, and he took off his pack and sat on the ground beside it with his back against the trunk of the tree. He took a deep breath and exhaled in a prolonged sigh as he tried to prepare himself mentally for what he knew would be a long night.

6:00 p.m.

Heller saw JT walking up the trail with his snowboard strapped to his pack and ran up the trail to meet him. "I was worried about you," Heller said. "I've been here for about an hour. You had a head start and were on your snowboard. I figured you'd be here well before me."

"I got lost coming down. I thought I was on the right track but came out below our campsite and had to hike back up to get here."

"Well, I'm glad to see you, bro," Heller said as he offered JT his flask of Jägermeister. JT took a healthy swig and said, "Where's Biter?"

"I don't know. I was hoping he was with you."

All of the color ran out of JT's face. "It's going to be dark in a few hours, and he's not here? Maybe he got lost like me. Or maybe the snow collapsed around the rocks where he left his skis, and he's trapped in a hole. He did find his skis, didn't he?"

Heller looked down. "I think he did."

"You don't know?"

"No," Heller said defensively. "I went down ahead of him and saw his skis in the rocks and thought he'd be fine. You got lost. Maybe he did too. Let's wait a little while before we start to freak out."

As they waited for their friend to return, JT and Heller gathered some wood and started a fire. As they sat across the fire from each other, they both had their eyes fixed on the trail, hoping and praying that their friend would suddenly appear. Finally Heller broke the silence. "If we're going to spend the night, we need the gear we left in Biter's car, and we need to get it before it's too dark for us to see."

"The car's locked, and Biter has the key."

"I know. Let's break the lock on the door with my ice axe."

JT and Heller held the ice axe between them a few feet from Biter's beat up Toyota and lunged forward, attempting to use the tool as a battering ram. On their first attempt, the point of the axe put a deep dent in the driver's side door about an inch to the right of the lock. The second attempt was slightly off to the left. The third try hit its mark but didn't do enough damage to free the door. Several more assaults were needed before the lock was totally obliterated, and the door acquiesced.

They retrieved their sleeping bags, put on some warm clothing and returned to the campfire. Neither spoke as they sat across from each other, staring at the flames. They understood the gravity of the situation and knew that with each passing hour the probability of a happy outcome was increasingly less likely. Each was reluctant to share his thoughts with the other as if uttering what they both feared would prove prophetic.

8:00 p.m.

Bathed in fog, Biter looked out at his surroundings and welcomed the encroaching darkness. It was the way he approached every impending unpleasant event in his life. The sooner an ordeal begins, the sooner it will be over and behind you. Bite the bullet, take your medicine and be done with it—that was his philosophy for handling bad situations. He wanted to fall asleep to escape the cold, but his mind was racing, and he was powerless to rein it in. He thought about his friends and worried that they were freaking out. They had seen the condition he had been in at Lunch Counter and knew he didn't have any warm clothes. Had they already contacted the authorities to let them know he was missing? Were they pissed at him for getting lost? If he survived and had to be rescued, what would the embarrassment of the news and media scrutiny be like? What if he died? What would happen to his stuff? He didn't have much of value, but what he did have, he wanted to go to the people he intended. He had never taken the time to make a will. How stupid! Why hadn't he made a will? Biter lay on his back and placed his pack on top of him in a futile attempt to get some protection from the cold.

10:00 p.m.

"We can't wait any longer," JT said. "We have to call the ranger. We need to get some help." JT and Heller walked to the neighboring campsites, looking for someone with a cell phone. At their second stop, they located a phone, and Heller made the call to the ranger station. JT stood next to him, listening intently. When Heller got off the phone, he said, "The ranger's on her way up."

As the two friends headed back to their campsite, JT said, "It's pitch black. They're not going to mount a search party tonight. They won't be able to do anything until morning at the earliest."

After about 30 minutes, they saw the headlights of a Forest Service truck approaching. They ran up to the vehicle as a female ranger in her mid-twenties stepped out of the cab. Her long, shiny black hair was tied in a ponytail and tucked neatly beneath her seemingly over-sized Smokey the Bear hat. Her unisex uniform couldn't hide her firm, shapely frame. "Hello, I'm Ranger Burns," she said as she extended her hand to JT. "Do you have a picture of the missing person?"

"I think I saw an old driver's license of his in our friend's glove box," JT answered as he ran to retrieve it from Biter's old beater. He rummaged through the contents in the compartment and finally found the expired license. The picture was obviously not recent. Biter was sporting a perm. JT handed the license to the ranger. "This is him, but he looks a lot different now."

"In what way?"

"He looks like Bob Ross in that picture."

"Who?"

"You know. That guy on TV who seems like he's on Prozac. He paints pictures of trees and mountains and stuff," JT explained.

"Our friend doesn't have curly hair now," Heller interjected.

The ranger was all business. "What condition was your friend in the last time you saw him?"

Heller glanced at JT. "He was soaking wet, drinking a beer, and shivering violently."

The ranger's light green eyes went cold, and her expression grew serious, betraying her concern. "Did he have additional clothing with him?"

"Just a pair of levis, I think," JT said grimly.

"I'm sure you realize it looks pretty serious. Hypothermia is a real concern, and we already have our hands full. We received a report of a missing teen on the mountain late this afternoon, and a recovery team will be leaving at dawn to look for this individual. We're tapped out as far as rescue personnel are concerned. We'll have to get some volunteers to come over from Yakima. I'm guessing the earliest we could mount a search party for your friend is in the late afternoon."

"We can't wait that long," JT objected. "We'll start looking for him ourselves as soon as it gets light."

"That's good. But keep us informed. We'll make sure you're included in the search party we'll be organizing. We'll contact you in the morning to get a status report and to give you an ETA for the rescue personnel from Yakima." The ranger reached into her truck and opened a map of the area on the bench seat. "Can you show me the location where you last saw your friend?"

Heller studied the map and pointed to the spot where he had last seen Biter. "I think it was here."

"The closest road to this location is Forest Service Road 8040," the ranger replied. "We'll have one of our staff members drive up and down this road tomorrow morning to look for your friend."

JT surveyed the map and ran his finger across the paper to a road some distance from the one the ranger had pointed out. "No, he'll come out here, Road 23. We came up that road. If Biter has a choice, he'll follow a trail that takes him to that road."

Shaking her head, the ranger said, "That's too far. It's got to be 20 miles or so from where you last saw your friend. No one has ever come out that far from where they were last sighted. Trust me. The road I've indicated is our best bet." The ranger folded up the map, threw it on the passenger's side of the seat and got in her truck. As she headed down the road, JT and Heller returned to the fire. JT placed his head in his hands and didn't say anything. Heller just stared at the flames.

2:00 a.m.

Biter removed his pack, stood up and walked a short distance from his resting spot to take a leak. His hands were numb, and he had a difficult time getting the zipper on his pants to descend. In fact, he noticed everything seemed to be more difficult. His muscles were stiff, and he felt a little unsteady. He caught himself tripping over his own feet, and his vision seemed to be a little suspect. He began to worry that the cold was finally taking its toll. When he returned to his resting spot, he once again lay on his back, took his baseball cap off his head and placed it over his face so when he exhaled, the precious warmth of his breath bathed his face before being wasted to the night. He placed his pack over him.

As the night slugged on, his body continued to shake like an old car struggling to start on a cold winter morning. He was so miserable that time slowed to a crawl. He tried not to look at his watch. He lay underneath his pack in the darkness with his eyes closed and tried to guess how much time had transpired since the last time he had checked. Surely, it must be at least an hour, he guessed. He looked at the neon green, illuminated face of his watch and saw it was only ten minutes since the last time he had checked. A minute seemed like an hour, and an hour seemed like an eternity. The paralysis of time made him much more aware of his involuntary reactions. He noticed his breathing was slow and shallow, and when he placed his index and middle fingers over his carotid artery to feel his pulse, he noticed his heart rate had fallen markedly as well.

As he lay on his back, Biter could hear a rustling sound on the ground behind him and felt droplets of moisture occasionally hitting the sides of his face. He guessed it was a shrew, scurrying around behind his head and spitting at him for invading its territory. As the frequency of the drops increased, he realized it was not the wrath of a small mammal but something more frightening...Rain!

His heart rate suddenly quickened, and he could feel his heart pounding in his head as he asked himself, "Rain! Jesus, could it get any worse?" Biter knew he was obviously confused and that his judgment was altered. He wondered if he was beginning to hallucinate. He felt incredibly weak and was tired beyond comprehension. Every cell in his body begged him to sleep, but he instinctively knew it would be his death sentence if he did. He had to stay awake if he was going to make it to morning. He knew he was on the verge of hypothermia. He tried not to panic but knew the constant shivering was taking its toll on his body. He wondered if he would be able to make it through the night. He started to take deep breaths as a way to calm his nerves. He was so incredibly tired that fighting the inclination to sleep was itself painful and tiring.

3:30 a.m.

JT was awakened by the sound of rain hitting the tarp above his head. He got out of his sleeping bag, crawled to the edge of the tarp and placed his hand outside. The rain hitting his hand was ice cold. JT recoiled at the thought of his friend out in such weather without the proper gear. He wanted to believe that Biter would survive the night, but he couldn't rid his mind of his last image of his friend shivering, wet and cold. He silently said a prayer and returned to his sleeping bag. He closed his eyes, but the pitter-patter of the unrelenting rain taunted him, preventing him from falling asleep. JT heard Heller rustling around in his sleeping bag. "Heller, are you awake?"

"Yeah, I can't sleep either."

"It's raining," JT said.

"I know," Heller responded. "If Biter dies, I'll be haunted by his ghost forever. I can't get the sight of him shivering out of my mind."

"Me neither. Why did we leave him like that?"

"We couldn't know he'd get lost," Heller said defensively. "It's nobody's fault."

"It doesn't matter," JT retorted. He waited for Heller to respond, but there was only silence. "It doesn't matter. We shouldn't have left him alone."

5:00 a.m.

Biter realized it had stopped raining. He took his pack off his chest and attempted to stand upright to survey his surroundings. He immediately fell to his knees. His arms and legs were now stiff and numb, and he realized that he had to move slowly to maintain his balance. Night was beginning to fade, and the fog was beginning to dissipate. Thick pillows of dense fog hovered near the ground amid the thinning curtain of gray, reminiscent of the smoke generated by dry ice when it's placed in water. The view reminded Biter of a set from a low budget horror movie, and he half expected to hear a wolf howl. Suddenly, he felt the hair stand up on the back of his neck as if someone was watching him. He turned around just in time to catch a glimpse of a bright, yellow-green man as he ducked behind a nearby fir tree.

Without thinking, Biter tried to run toward the tree to see if he could get a better view of whatever it was he had seen. His balance was still off-kilter, and he immediately fell facedown on the ground. As he struggled to get up, his peripheral vision caught movement to his left, and as he turned, he once again saw the figure of what looked like a man covered from head to foot in chartreuse paint just seconds before he, or it, disappeared behind another tree.

This time Biter didn't try to run. He maintained his position and just stared at the tree. After a minute or so, a green head, with short-cropped hair, appeared from behind the tree. The thick-lensed goggles or glasses he was wearing gave him a bulging, googly-eyed appearance. He smiled broadly and then slowly withdrew behind the trunk once again. Biter thought this figure looked strangely familiar, but he couldn't recall where he had seen him before.

He could barely contain himself. He was awash in a mixture of emotions. He wasn't afraid, despite the strangeness of the figure, and believed the figure was real and actually felt relieved that he was no longer alone. He was irritated by the incessant, nagging feeling we all get when we can't recall something we know is on the tip of our tongues. And, being from New Jersey, he was angry that someone, or something, was screwing with him. He wanted to run hell-bent for the tree, but instead, approached it slowly to keep from falling on his face. Upon arrival, he wrapped his head around the trunk, hoping to catch a glimpse of his antagonist. To his chagrin, he saw nothing but a frightened Douglas squirrel coming head first down the tree. The freaked out arboreal rodent let out a screech before leaping off the far side of the trunk and scurrying for safety.

Frustrated, Biter returned to the spot where he had left his gear. For the first time, he noticed that it was now light enough for him to begin his search for a way off the mountain. He was spent and had no stomach for carrying his heavy downhill ski gear with him. He decided to leave it behind, donned his backpack, and headed up the slope. He planned to retrace his steps until he came to the spot where he had separated from Heller.

However, once he left the cover of the trees, he saw that the rain had obliterated his tracks and had transformed the snow into a sheet of ice. Not wanting to abandon his only plan, he stubbornly continued his ascent. After about a quarter mile or so, his calves were on fire from kicking steps in the frozen snow, and he reluctantly turned around and once again headed downhill. To make himself feel that he was making some progress, he didn't retrace his steps but headed on a westward track as he made his descent.

After about a mile, he stopped to rest his legs. He wanted to take off his hiking boots but was afraid that his feet would swell and that he would have difficulty putting his boots back on. Instead, he rubbed his sore calves and snacked on the trail mix he still had in his pack. His throat was raw, and he had difficulty swallowing. He took a healthy swig of water to wash down the shards of chewed up peanuts and M&M's that stubbornly clung to his throat and then began to selectively consume the only ingredient in his homemade gorp that seemed to cause no problem—golden raisins.

The shriveled grapes seemed to restore at least a little energy, and he reluctantly forced himself to resume his trek after a respite of about fifteen minutes. As he slowly headed down the slope, he could see a large, hollow nurse log about 100 yards in front of him. The upper surface of the rotting, western red cedar was festooned with mosses, mushrooms, and ferns. Suddenly, the torso of the strange, green man lunged forward from the opening of the log, and Biter jumped back startled. The effortless way the green man moved was like toothpaste being squeezed from a tube. He spread his arms briefly before silently withdrawing back into the fallen timber.

Shaking, Biter made his way down to the log, hoping to get a closer look at the elusive figure. He stared into the opening, but there was nothing there. The image of the green man emerging from the log remained vivid in his mind, and it suddenly came to him where he had seen this figure before. It was in a toothpaste commercial he had seen countless times on TV as a child. The strange looking man was "Mr. Green!" In his mind, he could see him, coming out of the tube, and he could hear the accompanying jingle:

> You've a date tonight at eight,
> Everything has to be right.
> You want your breath to smell fresh
> And want your teeth ultra-white.
> Put your faith in Mr. Green
> For healthy, oral hygiene.
> Green's a teeth-cleaning machine.

The recollection should not have been a source of satisfaction. The fact that the green man he had seen was a hallucination should have caused him concern, but in his altered state, this reality seemed to escape him. His inability to recognize the strange, green man had been eating away at him, and finally identifying the figure had freed him of his obsession.

Pleased with himself, Biter shifted his focus from the fallen log and surveyed his surroundings. Under the dense forest canopy, the early morning light was still dim, but he could see a trail winding its way through the trees no more than twenty feet below him. A trail! His heart nearly exploded from his chest as he moved as fast as he felt capable down the slope to confirm his discovery.

When he reached the trail, he wanted to jump up and down in excitement, but his earlier clumsiness made him think better of this, and he let out a prolonged scream instead. The release of his pent-up stress felt wonderful. He savored the moment for a few minutes before heading west along the trail, which wound its way around the mountain.

Fueled by his adrenalin rush, he continued on his way at a steady pace for several miles before coming to a trifurcation in the trail. Each fork was marked by a road number, but there were no mile markers to indicate the relative lengths of each segment. Road 120 went off to the left. Road 23 was the middle fork, and Road 2329 went off to the right.

Biter and his friends had come up Road 23. The problem with this choice was that they had encountered a detour on their way up to the trailhead. If he chose this trail and came out above the detour, there would be no one on the road who could pick him up and take him to the ranger station. He knew there was no way he would be able to endure another night in the cold and that he would die of exposure if he came out on this road above the detour. Since he knew nothing about the other two choices, Biter felt he had no choice but to choose Road 23.

As he continued on his path, exhaustion overtook his enthusiasm and slowed his progress. He slugged along for another mile before coming to a bend in the trail. As he headed around the curve, the trail straightened out, and he could make out what looked like a billboard, partially hidden in the trees. There was a huge face on the sign, but he couldn't quite make it out from his vantage point. The presence of a billboard would mean he was near a highway! He became excited and picked up his pace. As he got closer, the visage on the large sign became discernible. The face Biter saw, staring back at him, looked like the computer-generated image you would get if you morphed a picture of Roseanne Barr with Queen Elizabeth II.

The strangeness of the figure was unsettling, and Biter ran toward the sign, seeking reassurance that what he was seeing was real. When he got within 100 yards of the billboard, it vanished in front of his eyes. Biter finally realized he was hallucinating, and while he found this unnerving, he was actually more upset by the stark realization that his hope of finding a highway nearby was dashed.

He continued on his way for another few miles before coming to a large clearing where the trail disappeared beneath a blanket of ice-encrusted snow. He panicked at the thought of losing his potential lifeline to civilization and ran to the center of the snowfield. He could feel his heart rate quickening as he slowly surveyed the tree line perimeter, looking for evidence of the trail's resumption beneath the protection of the trees. "Oh, God," Biter said to himself. "Don't do this to me. Don't make me have come all this way just to find a dead end."

As he nervously scanned the base of the circle of trees, he felt warmth on the back of his neck and turned around to witness the sun, climbing above the trees. The sun's warmth was rejuvenating. He closed his eyes, threw back his head, spread his arms, and arched his back in an effort to expose as much of his body to its life-giving rays as possible. He stood there for several minutes, soaking up the sun. With his eyes still closed, Biter smiled broadly. He felt like a spent car battery just put on a charger, and it felt wonderful!

The sun's rays had done more than just provide warmth. They had renewed his confidence and alleviated his anxiety. He opened his eyes, turned around and resumed his search for the trail. As he scanned the base of the trees in a clockwise direction, he detected movement in the canopy at the two o'clock position. His eyes shot upward. Twenty feet above the forest floor, Biter saw what appeared to him to be a full-sized, gray horse. Its long, slender legs were wrapped tightly around the trunk of a tree. The body and neck of the animal looked like a real horse, but its head, and especially its muzzle, were exaggerated and cartoon-like, more reminiscent of "Quick Draw McGraw" than a real animal.

Although it appeared to him as real as his other hallucinations, Biter now realized this apparition was only a figment of his imagination. He knew it would disappear like the others, and this realization was the turning point in his recovery. As he approached the fir where he thought he had seen the horse, he looked up, and saw nothing but a long stretch of furrowed bark, interrupted by an occasional explosion of branches. He smiled broadly as he raised his head skyward and laughed heartily. The realization that he was now back in reality pleased him, and, as he lowered his gaze, he saw the trail ten feet in front of him! He had found his lifeline! His heart soared, and he let out a howl of elation. There was no guarantee that this trail would take him back to his friends, but it gave him hope and, at this stage, that was everything.

12 noon

JT and Heller were making their way back to camp after spending the morning searching for Biter. They had gotten up before first light to look for their friend. They had hiked above the tree line where they had a clear view of the rocks where Biter had left his skis. They had scoured the ridge, looking for his tracks, but the rain the night before had erased any evidence of the path he had taken.

They were now on their way back to their campsite. As they made their descent, they were both extremely tired from a night of fitful sleep and in a state of nervous depression. Not knowing what had happened to their friend made them imagine the worst. Had he skied over a snow bridge, which collapsed, trapping him in an icy coffin? Had he skied off a cliff? Had he broken a leg and frozen to death? The various scenarios played out individually in their minds as they headed downhill without speaking.

Finally Heller broke the silence. "Hey, maybe Biter's back at camp, waiting for us. If he made it through the night, he would have started hiking at the crack of dawn like we did. He could be there now."

"Yeah," JT said, eager to grasp at any straw of hope they could muster. "Let's hurry back."

As they headed down the long series of switchbacks that led to their camp, they heard the faint but unmistakable sound of a helicopter approaching. As the harsh clack-clack-clack-clack sound of the copter's blades grew in intensity, they looked skyward and caught fleeting glimpses of a helicopter as it flew above the forest canopy.

"I bet they're looking for Biter," JT said.

"Yeah, I bet you're right," Heller agreed. "Let's get back to camp. Maybe the ranger is there with some news."

With renewed hope, they made their descent. As they got closer to camp, they picked up their pace and were nearly on a run by the time they made the final turn where they could see their campsite.

"Look," Heller said excitedly. "There's the ranger's truck!"

The pair ran down the trail, eager for some news. As they approached the Forest Service truck, a tall, lanky ranger stepped out of the vehicle, grabbed his hat off the seat and placed it on his head. Extending his hand, he said, "I'm Ranger Dooley. Are you the friends of the missing person?"

"Yes," Heller said as he shook the ranger's hand.

"We saw a helicopter when we were searching for our friend," JT interjected. "Did you find him?"

"No. I was hoping he might have made it back to camp by now. That's one of the reasons I'm here—"

Heller cut him off. "Is the copter we saw searching for our friend?"

"Unfortunately, no," the ranger replied stoically. As he said this, his gray eyes lost their light, and Heller and JT knew instantly that the next words out of his mouth would not be good news. "The helicopter you saw was a Medevac helicopter. It was evacuating the body of the other person we were searching for.

The search party that left this morning found the body a few hours ago. The cause of death looks like a fall. We think the person fell about 200 feet to his death."

Heller and JT glanced at each other without speaking. "The other reason I'm here is to ask you to remain at camp until the search and rescue team gets here," the ranger said. "We want you to take us up to the last place you saw your friend. I know you've been searching all morning, and we want you to rest so you have enough energy to take us there."

"Yes, we want to help," JT said. "We took some hot soup with us this morning, hoping to find our friend, but we couldn't even find his tracks."

"The rain last night destroyed everything," Heller offered.

"I know," the ranger said. "Just stay here and I'll keep you abreast of what's going on. I assure you I'll let you know right away when we know something—good or bad." The ranger got back into his truck and headed down the road.

JT and Heller followed his progress until his vehicle disappeared from sight. Even though it wasn't cold, they spent time gathering wood and building a fire in an effort to keep busy and avoid dwelling on the negative thoughts that were most pregnant in their minds.

3:00 p.m.

To Biter, it seemed like he had been hiking forever. He didn't know how many miles he had traveled, but he knew it was considerable. The sun's rays had warmed his core and renewed his energy, but the blanket of blue sky he had enjoyed for most of the day had gradually been broken by a patchwork of cumulus clouds. For hours the trail had seemed to maintain its relative position on the mountain. For every downhill stretch Biter traveled, there seemed to be an equal section of trail that climbed upward. Now, for the first time, the trail started to take a noticeably downward course.

As Biter made his descent, the trail also seemed to sink deeper into the ground. Like a microcosmic Grand Canyon, the path slowly subsided, and the sides of the trail gradually grew in height as he traveled downward. The earthen walls gave the surrounding vegetation an exaggerated importance. Thickets of snowberries, thimbleberries and an occasional outcropping of devil's club rose overhead like miniature trees. Roots routinely thrust their way out of the reddish-brown soil walls only to turn back on themselves and return to their rightful place. As he continued on his way, Biter felt like a Hobbit and savored the almost mystical quality of his surroundings.

While Biter was consumed with his version of Middle Earth, the cumulus clouds that had earlier hidden the sun had risen in height, and it now started to rain. The first droplets that hit Biter's face returned him to the reality of the present. He was still lost, the afternoon was waning, and it was starting to rain! He knew he couldn't survive another night in the cold, and he quickened his pace.

As he made his way down the trail's switchbacks, his view of his surroundings gradually improved, and he could see a considerable distance downhill. Suddenly, he saw a figure making his way up the trail. He caught a fleeting glimpse of a blond-haired man before the stranger disappeared from view. He fixed his gaze on the trail, waiting for the man to reappear. As the figure came around a bend in the trail, he saw the face of the man. It was JT!

As he ran down the trail to meet his friend, his mind kicked into overdrive. How could JT have known he was on this trail? Was it another hallucination? His initial excitement plummeted as the realization arose that what he wanted to see might just be another illusion. This sobering thought stopped him dead in his tracks, and he struggled to get a better view of the approaching figure.

As he waited for the man to reappear, his heart rate quickened. He stared at the first place along the trail where he thought he could possibly get his next glimpse of the man. As he waited, his level of fear rose and his thoughts raced. The man should have gotten to this spot by now! Why isn't he there? Has he disappeared like everything else I've seen today? Am I seeing what I desperately want, rather than what actually exists?

He could hear his heart pounding in his ears. Just as he was getting ready to run down the trail, a yellow lab came into view followed shortly behind by a tall, blond stranger. The man wasn't JT, but he was real! He wasn't a figment of Biter's imagination!

Biter ran down the trail, and the lab raced forward to greet him, its tail wagging in excitement. Biter knelt down and grabbed the dog around his neck, hugging him as he would a long, lost friend. He then stood up and walked to the approaching figure, extending his hand. "Hello, I've been missing for a day now. I'm sure everybody's looking for me. Would you mind taking me to the ranger station?"

"Sure, no problem," the man answered. "I was just about ready to turn around anyway, with the rain starting. I was just taking my dog out for some exercise. I didn't have any destination in mind."

4:10 p.m.

Heller and JT were sitting around the fire as the Forest Service truck made its way up to their campsite. They got up to greet the ranger as he exited his vehicle.

"The search and rescue team from Yakima will be here within an hour," the ranger said. "I just wanted to give you guys a heads-up so you would be ready to go when they get here."

"We've been ready all day," JT replied.

Heller thought this sounded negative so he attempted to soften its impact. "We know you're doing all you can, and we appreciate it. It's just difficult sitting here and waiting, when our friend is out there."

"I understand completely," the ranger said. "I know how I would feel if one of my friends was missing. You guys have been through hell the last twenty-four hours. No explanation is necessary. We just appreciate your help and patience. I'll see you in about an hour." The ranger shook hands with Heller and JT, got in his vehicle, and headed down the road.

JT and Heller returned to the fire. "I hate this waiting," JT said. "I want to be doing something."

"I know, brother," Heller agreed. "I feel the same way."

4:12 p.m.

Biter entered the ranger station and walked up to the counter. The girl at the desk looked up to greet him. "Hello, I've been missing for a day," Biter said. "And I think you're looking for me. I'm Greg Starypan."

Ranger Burns was standing behind the receptionist and overheard the disheveled camper's words. "That's an understatement! We're just getting ready to mount a search party to look for you. Do you need medical attention?"

"No, I'm fine," Biter assured her. "I just want to get back to my friends."

"We'll take you up there right away. Would you like some coffee or something while I get the truck?"

Biter wanted to ask for a beer, but he thought better of this and answered, "I'd love a cup."

4:20 p.m.

JT and Heller sat around the campfire as they watched the approach of the Forest Service vehicle with increasing trepidation. They had seen the ranger just ten minutes before. They both instinctively knew that his return meant that Biter's fate was now known. The ranger either had the good news they desperately wanted to hear or the dreaded news they secretly believed was the likely outcome of this long ordeal.

"I can't take it," JT said. "You go up and talk to him."

Heller stood up and walked slowly toward the Forest Service vehicle. To JT, time slowed to a crawl as he watched Heller's progress. He felt like he was underwater. In slow motion, he saw Heller approach the Forest Service vehicle as the ranger got out of the truck. He saw the ranger talking to Heller, and then he saw his friend turn back to him.

"Biter's alive!" Heller shouted as he ran back to JT. "Another hiker picked him up and took him to the ranger station! He got there just about the same time the ranger last saw us. He's alive! Can you believe it? He's alive!"

JT ran up, grabbed Heller around the waist and lifted him as high as he could. They both laughed hysterically as they hugged each other and savored the moment.

4:30 p.m.

Biter looked out the window of the Forest Service truck as Ranger Burns drove him up the winding road that would reunite him with his friends. "When your friends called to report you missing, I was having dinner with a friend. After the call, I went outside, and the weather was deteriorating. I said to my friend, 'Let this be a lesson for us. Never go out on a hike without the proper gear. I don't care how long you think you'll be gone.'"

"I know," Biter agreed. "I feel stupid. I've been hiking and climbing for years, and I know better. I just thought we were going on a day hike."

"That's probably what most people who've died on this mountain would say. You were very lucky. I think someone was watching over you."

"My friends are probably going to be angry with me," Biter said. "We were supposed to leave yesterday."

Ranger Burns was incredulous. "Are you kidding me? They're so incredibly happy that you're alive!"

As they made the final stretch to the campground, Biter could see his friends sitting around the campfire. Upon seeing the Forest Service truck, JT and Heller jumped up and ran toward the approaching vehicle. They both grabbed Biter as soon as he exited the truck and gave him a long hug.

When his two friends finally released their grasp, Biter walked over to the truck and thanked the ranger for her help. She had a big smile on her face. "And you thought your buddies were going to be mad at you," she said. "Truthfully, this wasn't the ending I had envisioned for this story last night when your friends called to tell me you were missing, so it looks like neither of us got it right. I can't tell you how happy I am it ended this way." As she turned her vehicle around and proceeded down the road, Biter once again turned back to his friends.

"Look at him," Heller exclaimed. "He doesn't look any different than the last time we saw him!"

There was a remarkable moment of silence when all three men stood motionless. They all knew their reunion was something for which they had all prayed desperately, but none had believed would be the final outcome.

Finally, JT broke the silence. Smiling broadly with tears welling in his eyes, he extended his right hand. "Biter, I can't ever look at you the same way again."

Biter grabbed his friend's hand.

"I'm serious," JT said as he covered their right hands with his left and squeezed firmly.

"I know," Biter said as he wrapped his free arm around his friend and hugged him. "I know."

When the two friends had finished reliving their Mt. Adams experience, JT got up from his chair and went downstairs to the garage to get more beer. As Biter waited for his friend to return, he reflected on JT's comment: *Biter, I can't ever look at you the same way again.* Biter understood instinctively that the fact that he had survived his ordeal on the mountain held a larger importance for his friend because, at that time, JT was still struggling to cope with an event that had changed his life forever.

NINE

Two years before the Mt. Adams experience, JT and his longtime girlfriend Wendy were in his car traveling down Highway US-95 on their way to Las Vegas. Their trip to the NASCAR race was an annual ritual. It was their one brief opportunity in late winter to trade the incessantly cold, rainy weather of the Oregon Coast for the sunny and still mild, daytime temperatures of the Nevada desert.

Wendy was a tall, blue-eyed beauty with long, curly chestnut-brown hair and a radiant smile. She and JT had been going together since high school and loved each other intensely, but they both were strong-willed and very different in so many ways. Wendy needed a large number of friends around her to prove to her that she was popular. JT, on the other hand, was a more private person and comfortable in his own skin. He only had a few, really close friends, and this was the way he liked it.

Wendy was a planner and was always projecting a few years down the road, making decisions based on what she wanted that future to look like. JT, in contrast, was a free spirit, who was content just taking things as they came.

Wendy was also very protective of JT, and this was the source of many of their arguments. She viewed her overriding concern for his welfare as a sign of her love for him. He saw her intervention as proof that she was trying to "smother him," and he thought that's exactly what she was doing now.

"You've been driving for several hours," Wendy nagged. "You were up late last night, playing roulette, and I know you must be tired. Why don't you let me drive for a while?"

"I'm fine," JT responded. "I work in a bar. I'm used to being up late."

"But you're not drinking when you're bartending," Wendy insisted. "You had a lot to drink last night."

"And you didn't?"

"Not as much as you. And I went to bed several hours before you got back to the room."

"Okay," JT said in frustration, as he pulled the car over to the shoulder. "Have it your way. You can drive, and I'll try to take a nap in the back seat if I can get comfortable."

Wendy got behind the wheel as JT hopped in the back seat and lay down. "If you start to feel tired, wake me up," he said.

"Don't worry, I'm fine," Wendy assured him. "Just try to get some sleep."

That was the last thing JT remembered before the accident.

When he woke up in the hospital, he learned that the love of his life, his dear Wendy, was dead. An old man, traveling northward, had a stroke and had come over into their lane and hit them head-on. Both the old man and Wendy died instantly. The only reason JT had survived was because he was lying down in the back of the car. The impact had sent him sailing into the front seats and knocked him unconscious. He had a broken arm, some cracked ribs and was badly bruised, but he was still alive.

As soon as he heard the terrible news, Biter called JT and offered to come down to spend time with him. To his dismay, JT refused, thanking him for the offer, but saying he needed time to be alone. Biter tried contacting him repeatedly for weeks after that, but his calls went unanswered. He knew his friend was hurting deeply. He knew how much JT loved Wendy, and he wanted desperately to help his friend, but he didn't know what to do. With each passing day without a call from JT, Biter feared the worst.

Each time the phone rang, Biter struggled to cope with two competing scenarios. He wanted to believe the call would be good news, that it would be JT, telling him he was OK and asking him to come down to spend some time with him. He knew, however, there was an even likelihood that the call would be the dreaded news he secretly feared—that JT had been unable to cope with his grief and had taken his own life.

Several months after the accident, Biter got a call from JT. He acted like nothing had happened and that no time had passed at all. "What are you doing this weekend, Biter? I was hoping you'd want to come down and spend some time on the river."

Biter jumped at the offer. "Yes, I'd love to."

"Great. I'll see you when you get here," JT said as he hung up the phone.

Biter was ecstatic that he had heard from JT, but he was bothered by the brevity of the call.

As Biter drove down Little Switzerland Road, he realized he didn't know what to say to his friend. He wanted to tell JT how incredibly sorry he was for his loss, but he knew any words he could muster would pale in comparison to the way he actually felt. He also didn't want to inadvertently make JT relive the horror of that day. He decided to say nothing and follow JT's lead. When JT opened the door, Biter just gave him a big hug.

"Good to see you too, cousin," JT said. "Bring your stuff in and take a seat on the deck. I'll get us a couple of beers from the garage."

When JT arrived with the beers, Biter said, "It's good to see you. I was worried about you."

"I know. I'm sorry I didn't return your calls, but I didn't feel up to talking to anyone. I hope you understand."

"No need to apologize. I'm just glad you're OK."

JT looked out over the river and didn't say anything. Biter immediately regretted his statement. "I don't mean OK, I—"

JT cut him off. "Biter you've been walking on eggshells since you got here. I know you're afraid that I'm fragile right now, but I'm not made of glass, and I'm not going to shatter to pieces in front of your eyes. Be yourself. That's the person I want to spend time with right now. You and I both know I'm not OK. A part of me died that day when Wendy was taken from me, and I've spent the last few months struggling with whether I should even try to cope with the loss or let it consume me. My invitation for you to come down this weekend should tell you what decision I arrived at."

Biter was afraid to say anything for fear of making his friend feel even worse, but he had to know. "What made you decide to go on?"

JT took a healthy swig of his beer and laughed as he stared down into the fishpond immediately in front of his L-shaped deck. "Do you see that goldfish near the surface next to that lily pad?"

"Which one?"

"The big white one with the red and black markings on his back."

"Oh, yeah, I see the one you're talking about," Biter said.

"That's Duke," Biter heard his friend say. He gave JT a strange look. "Do you give all of your goldfish names?"

"No, he's the only one that has a name. He's special." JT finished his beer and got up to go to the garage. "This story will take a little time," JT explained, "so I need to get another beer first."

Biter chugged what beer was remaining in his glass and jumped up. "No, let me get it. I want to hear your story about this special fish."

JT laughed, handed Biter his glass and sat back down. "Thanks, bro. I'll be here when you get back."

Biter filled their glasses and hurried back to the deck. When he sat down, JT took a healthy swig of his beer and started his story. "A few months before the accident, the river flooded, and I was so caught up in trying to get everything out of my garage that I didn't have time to deal with my fish. I figured they would either hunker down at the bottom of the pond or be swept down the river. Then a huge western red cedar root ball went sailing down the river and took out our community water system."

Biter wanted to make sure he understood what JT was talking about. "Your water line is that white PVC pipe that's suspended over the river about a quarter mile from here?"

"Exactly," JT said. "The root ball took it out, so we had no running water. I had to carry muddy water from the river to gravity flush my toilet. I kept a five-gallon bucket of water outside the door near my downstairs bathroom just for this purpose.

The next morning, after the river had receded, my neighbor Dave came over to see if I was OK, and we walked around my house to inspect for any damage. I saw a few of my goldfish in the front yard, lying in the soil under an apple tree. When I picked up one of the fish, it started to move. 'It's alive!' I yelled as I ran to the door, grabbed the bucket and placed the fish in the water. I took the bucket down to the apple tree, searched around the yard, found two more fish and placed them in the container.

I took the bucket to the back of the house. The water was full of mud, so I couldn't see the fish and had to feel around in the water to find them. Eventually, I was able to grab all three and throw them back in the pond. I returned the bucket to my door so I could use the water on my next trip to the latrine.

A few hours later, I went to take a dump and used the water in the bucket to flush the toilet. As I poured the water into the bowl, two fish sailed out of the bucket and went down the drain. I knew I had only retrieved three fish, so I went over to my neighbor's house and told him what had happened. Dave said he had also picked up two fish in my front yard and placed them in the bucket as well."

Biter couldn't help himself and began laughing heartily.

"It wasn't funny," JT said, obviously annoyed. "I felt awful! After a few beers with my neighbor, I had to the take a whiz. I grabbed another bucket of water from the river and headed for the can. As I started to piss, a goldfish swam up from the bottom of the toilet and looked up at me. One of the two fish hadn't been flushed after all! I ran outside and got my fish net and tried to scoop him up, but he retreated down the hole." JT started to laugh and shake his head. "My square net was just too big. I had to put on a rubber glove and stick my hand down the toilet to fish him out. The poor little guy tried to get away and jumped straight up out of the bowl!"

JT got down on one knee and lifted his hands in the air as if he was struggling to catch the fish. "I'm trying to help you, I said. Finally, when I caught him, I put the fish in the bucket and took him over to show my neighbor before I put him back in the pond. We both had a good laugh and decided we'd start calling him Dookey. Over time, I've shortened it and just call him Dook."

Biter was laughing so hard his stomach hurt. "So his name's not Duke, it's Dook."

JT understood what Biter meant, but he still had to bust his chops. He took a drink and asked, "Biter, are you going to let me finish my story or are you going to keep interrupting me?"

"Go," Biter said.

JT started laughing as well and took another drink. "After the flood, there was mud everywhere, and we spent several days cleaning up the mess. That fish was the only thing that gave my neighbor and me something to laugh about.

Over the past few months, I've spent a lot of time out here on the deck drinking too much and feeling way too sorry for myself. Every time I threw pellets into the pond to feed the fish, and Dook came up to the surface and looked at me, I had to laugh. I swear it was the one thing that kept me going. I know it sounds crazy, but I think that fish saved my life. If he could survive being shit on and pissed on, then I could too."

Biter bit his lip and struggled to keep his composure. He looked down into his beer. He didn't know what to say.

JT didn't seem to notice. "The fish that hunkered down in the pond and didn't leave had played it safe and survived, but they traded their one chance for an awesome adventure for security. Dook, on the other hand, took a chance." JT chuckled as he took the time to remember the moment. "Yeah, so it didn't work out so well. But can you imagine what it must have been like going from a 250-gallon pond to a river that was overflowing its banks?" JT was nearly in tears thinking about it. "It must have been awesome!"

JT took another drink. "Biter, we like to think we have control over our lives, but then something happens to remind us that that's not the way life works. The disappointments, the dead ends, the unexpected twists and turns that alter our path, and, yes, even the deepest, darkest moments in our lives—they're all learning experiences. We can either let ourselves be swept away by the events we are subjected to or we can struggle to rise above them. I realized it's how we react to the experiences in our lives that ultimately define us. I wasn't going to be one of the goldfish that hunkered down in the pond. I was going to live the rest of my life to the fullest. I know that's what Wendy would have wanted me to do."

Biter knew that JT was still struggling to deal with his broken heart, but he no longer had any doubt that his friend would survive.

After Wendy died, Biter understood that JT couldn't stand to lose another person in his life for whom he cared about so much, and after the Mt. Adams experience, Biter knew that JT could never look at him the same again. If he had died on Mt. Adams, Biter knew it would have sent JT over the edge. His survival, like Dook's, gave JT hope and the motivation to continue. It was the seminal moment that sealed their enduring friendship.

JT returned from the garage with their barleywine, and this brought Biter back to the present. Returning to the Mt Adams experience, he said to JT, "Yeah, you couldn't ever look at me the same way again. Do you know how long that lasted?"

"What do you mean?"

"Maybe four or five months after the Mt. Adams trip, you and I were at the Kirkwood ski resort in South Lake Tahoe. It was late in the afternoon, and you convinced me to go off trail with you. Do you remember that?"

JT looked annoyed. "Yeah, so what's your point?"

"We came to an ice wall. We threw our gear down and had to climb down the wall. When we got down and retrieved our gear from the snow, a binding on one of my rental skis was missing. It was getting dark, and the fog was settling in. I had to ski down on one ski. You said you'd see me at the bottom and snowboarded down. Do you remember that?"

"Of course," JT said.

"When I finally got down, you were nowhere to be found. I checked all the lifts and then returned my skis. When I got back to your truck, you were smoking a joint. When I told you I had been looking for you at all the lifts, you said, 'I knew you'd make it down.'"

"I did know you'd make it down," JT insisted. "You survived a cold, rainy night on Mt. Adams with nothing but a wet T-shirt and jeans. A little fog and one ski was nothing."

Put in those terms, Biter had to agree JT was right. They touched their glasses in a silent toast.

TEN

Biter had been living at JT's home for several months and had experienced no success in finding a good-paying position. With his funds completely tapped out, he had no recourse but to take a job as a dishwasher at a local restaurant while he continued his search for more lucrative and rewarding employment. He hated the job, not because he viewed it as beneath him, but because it made him feel like he was going backwards in his life.

He had been a dishwasher when he was sixteen years old. At that time, he was thankful for the work, or more accurately, the paycheck it provided and the expansion in his personal freedom that having his own money represented. But he was now thirty-three and being forced to take a job as a dishwasher at this stage in his life was a difficult reality to accept.

Biter stacked the food-encrusted plates and silverware into faded, green plastic trays and placed them on the black conveyor belt that was being swallowed by the stainless steel dishwasher. He looked over at his co-worker, who was removing the clean dishes from the opposing side of the steam-belching, metal box.

Biter's fellow dishwasher, Mickey, was a tall, skinny man in his late twenties. His thinning, light blond hair was buzz cut to an extreme, giving his head the appearance of a sun-starved, newly sprouted Elmer Fudd Chia Pet. To Biter, Mickey was withdrawn and edgy. He frequently called in sick and, even when he did show up, was habitually late for work. Because of this, Biter viewed him as lazy and had no patience or respect for the man.

Had he known that Mickey was a veteran of the Gulf War, who suffered from post-traumatic stress disorder, he might have had more empathy. However, without being privy to this information, all Biter knew was that each day Mickey didn't show up, or was late for work, it made his life more difficult for he was then left to staff the dishroom alone. He resented the burden this put on him, and his disdain for his co-worker grew in intensity each time Mickey was a no show.

Mickey's biggest detractor, however, wasn't Biter but the restaurant's hostess, Rose. She was a portly woman who frequently wore clothes that were too small for her robust size. The buttons on her blouse were always overworked to the point of exhaustion, and her jet-black hair was equally constrained in extremely tight, unnatural curls. To make her appearance even less appealing, she applied her makeup as if she believed each eighth-of-an-inch of foundation took ten years off her perceived age. To Biter, her heavily applied, bright red lipstick made her lips look like the inflamed ass of a baboon. She reminded him of a bloated version of the 17th century French philosopher, Descartes. He smiled to himself as he mentally twisted this man's most notable philosophical statement to apply to Rose: I'm fat, therefore I am.

For some reason, Rose got perverse pleasure in deriding Mickey in front of the other kitchen staff on a daily basis. Mickey hated her for this, and it was all he could do to keep from killing her. Mickey's nickname for Rose was "Queen." Although Biter never asked Mickey why he called her this, he himself could see a resemblance between Rose and the Queen of Hearts in Lewis Carroll's *Alice in Wonderland* and assumed this was likely Mickey's inspiration for the appellation.

Unlike Biter and Rose, the restaurant's head cook, Sarah, personally harbored no ill will for Mickey, but she was a troublemaker who lived to cause dissension in the kitchen and saw Mickey as the catalyst she could use to accomplish her goal. She knew Biter hated his position and that Mickey made his job even more unpalatable.

Of Irish descent, Sarah was a woman in her mid-fifties with bright red hair, rosy cheeks and soft, cream-colored skin. While she was someone Biter should have seen as a manipulator and avoided, he was drawn to her because he felt she shared some of the same traits he saw in himself and for which he was most proud. She was demonstrative, fiercely independent and not afraid to fight for what she thought was right.

She, of course, used their friendship to further her own ends and did everything she could to cause Biter's and Mickey's relationship to fester for no other reason than to keep things in the kitchen interesting. When Biter complained that Mickey was always coming up with some lame excuse to disappear from the dishroom for an hour or more at time, Sarah not only agreed but also offered the inflammatory observation that Mickey was a user.

"I know he comes off as being loopers," she told Biter, "but I think he exaggerates his health problems to get out of work. You are left alone in the dishroom for long periods while Mickey gets to sit on his arse. It's not right, and you shouldn't stand for it."

Biter, of course, agreed with Sarah's assessment and, with her encouragement, made up his mind he would find the right time to do something about it. As fate would have it, that didn't take long. The perfect opportunity arose a little more than a week later. Mickey's latest excuse for escaping from the dishroom for prolonged periods was a bad case of hemorrhoids.

The employee's bathroom was in an alcove immediately behind the kitchen. To get there from the dishroom, Mickey had to cross Sarah's path. She could sense something was wrong, and though she didn't find conversing with him especially interesting, she let her curiosity get the best of her on his third trip to the john in an hour.

"Mickey, what's up? You've been hitting the shitter all day. Got the scutters?"

"No, hemorrhoids. I never had them this bad before. Do you have anything in the kitchen that would help me?"

Sarah searched the supplies in the cabinet above her head, grabbed a box of cornstarch off the upper shelf and handed it to Mickey. "Wipe some of this on your arse and be on your way."

Mickey shuffled to the bathroom, clutching the box close to his side. Once inside, he locked the door behind him, undid his pants, and collapsed on the broken toilet seat. He pulled a long length of toilet paper off the roll, reached across the small, discolored sink, and turned on the cold water. He placed the wad of paper underneath the spigot, wetting the TP beyond the limits of its absorbency. As he withdrew the watery mass of paper and applied it to the inflamed area, he savored the fleeting moment of relief the cold water provided. Mickey dispensed several more scrolls of paper and repeated the process. When this ritual seemed to have outlived its usefulness, he wiped his butt and grabbed the box of cornstarch off the edge of the sink and poured a healthy mound of the soft, white powder into his right hand. As he applied the cornstarch to his butt, he also carelessly dispensed a healthy amount of the powder on the floor and also on his black jeans, which were lying in a heap around his ankles. He then stood up, raised his trousers, and cinched his belt.

As Mickey exited the bathroom, Sarah could barely contain herself. The sight of Mickey's jeans plastered with cornstarch would have been funny enough, but he had forgotten to zip his fly. With neither boxers nor briefs to conceal it, Mickey's manhood was clearly visible through the open zipper. Sarah bit her tongue to keep from laughing and pretended to look busy as Mickey returned the box of cornstarch and headed back to the dishroom.

Rose caught a glimpse of Mickey out of the corner of her eye as he walked past the doorway to the dining room. "Mickey, we need some dishes out here," she barked. "Be quick about it."

He rankled at having to take orders from this witch. "Keep your panties on," he said, under his breath and then raised the level of his response, "I'll get there as soon as I can."

As Mickey hurried into the dishroom to get the plates, Biter turned to confront him, intending to scold him for his long absence, but he noticed Mickey's fly was undone and didn't want to do anything to give him time to stop and realize his error. Biter motioned to the large stack of clean plates. "Take those plates out to the dining room and put an end to Rose's bitching."

"I'd like to hit Queen across the face with a two-by-four repeatedly," Mickey said, "but that would probably just improve her looks." He grabbed the plates, turned around, and headed for the dining room.

"Go get her Mick," Biter yelled as he laughed hysterically and watched him leave. He wanted to run after Mickey to see what the outcome would be but waited until his co-worker had entered the dining room before hurrying to the entrance to witness the spectacle.

Mickey marched into the dining room with the huge stack of plates and leaned back broadly in order to lift the plates high enough to place them on the spring-loaded, plate-serving table. As he did so, his flaccid penis fell out of his open zipper.

Rose noticed this immediately and let her inclination to bust Mickey's balls overtake her better judgment. "Mickey, stick your dick back in your pants! Zip it up," she shrieked. Something that might have gone unnoticed was now the focus of the entire dining room.

Mickey could hear people laughing, and his embarrassment was all consuming. He quickly zipped up his fly and ran from the dining room, screaming, "Shut up Queen!"

Biter ran back to the dishroom and was laughing so hard he was nearly in tears. Mickey wasn't far behind him.

"Flying a little low there weren't you, Mick?"

"Fuck you," Mickey replied.

"No, screw you! You've been missing in action all day, and I'm tired of it. It's my turn to sit on my ass. I'll be back after my break," Biter said as he started to exit the dishroom.

"What are you doing? We've got this banquet going on," Mickey said. "You know we'll be buried in a shitload of dishes. I need your help!"

"Where were you when I needed yours? You can handle it. You're a big boy, Mick!"

Biter went outside, unlocked his car door, plopped down in his driver's seat, and put an Alice in Chains disc in his CD player. As he listened to "Bleed the Freak," he thought about his fellow co-worker and wondered if it were possible for Mickey to be any more screwed up than he already was. As this song and the ones that followed played out, he allowed himself to be caught up in the music and put Mickey out of his mind.

While Biter enjoyed his break, Mickey was going crazy in the dishroom. Stacks and stacks of dirty dishes and glasses, filled with food-encrusted silverware, marched down the conveyor belt from the dining room like an invading army. Mickey tried to keep up with the onslaught, but couldn't work fast enough. As the mound of dirty dishes grew, the china, glasses, and silverware started to spread out in all directions. Eventually, the entire stainless steel countertop was overrun, and plates, cups, glasses, and silverware cascaded over the edge and fell to the floor.

The high-pitched, unsettling sounds of breaking glass and china heightened Mickey's already overloaded stress level, triggering a traumatic event that he had been forced to relive countless times before. He shut his eyes futilely as if this would erase the scene playing out in his head and walked backwards to get as far away from the offending noise as possible. When his back made contact with the opposing wall, he slid down to the floor, pulled his legs up, and buried his head in his knees.

When the CD ended, Biter exited his car and walked back to the restaurant. Upon entering the dishroom, he was struck by the eerie feeling that the dishes had risen up in revolt and that he was now in occupied territory. His eyes scanned the glass and ceramic carnage in disbelief and keyed up on the broken figure huddled on the floor. He ran over to see if Mickey was OK and started to panic when there was no response when he shook him and shouted his name.

ELEVEN

A young, scrawny GI with a blond buzz cut regained consciousness amid a hailstorm of sand, glass, and metal fragments. A cacophony of familiar but alarming sounds—the monotonous drone of a landing Blackhawk helicopter; the incessant, strident sounds of ambulance sirens; the impersonal, rather alien-sounding radio communications of rescue personnel and the unsettling screams of human suffering—added to the assault on his senses.

The impact of the scud missile had destroyed his barracks and taken out the electrical grid. His pupils struggled to handle the extremes of surrounding, jet-black, desert darkness and the isolated, blinding light of the headlamps of rescue vehicles.

He tried to make sense of the thin beams of constantly moving light that illuminated the obliterated fiberglass insulation that floated through the air like bloated fireflies. He suddenly realized that the light was coming from the flashlights of fellow soldiers, frantically searching the rubble for the dead and wounded.

He remembered that he had been working out with some of his buddies outside the barracks. He recalled hearing the alarm sirens. He suddenly realized that his best friend, Sam Romero, had been inside the barracks, relaxing on his cot, when the surface-to-surface missile hit. He jumped up and ran into the mangled mass of steel and corrugated metal to find his friend.

Scattered on the ground amid the wreckage were the disembodied limbs and mutilated bodies of his fellow soldiers. Crimson pools of blood lay everywhere like puddles after a downpour. He helped several GIs lift a ten-foot section of steel girder off a soldier trapped underneath. To his horror, the lifeless body was that of his friend. The right side of Sam's skull was crushed, and his body was covered in blood. The sight of his friend's disfigured body was more than he could bear. He cried out in anguish as he dropped to his knees and pulled his friend's lifeless body toward him. He held him tightly to his chest as rivulets of his friend's blood mixed with his own tears and ran down his T-shirt. He stood up and carried his friend's body from the broken building.

Like every other soldier, he and Sam had talked about their mortality and what they wanted the other to do if they were the one to make the ultimate sacrifice. He remembered Sam, looking at a picture of his wife that he kept in his wallet and saying, "Mick, if I die, you have to tell Susan how much I love her. Tell her I told you to say: Until the end of time." Mickey understood the significance of this single sentence. Sam had explained that he and Susan had been high school sweethearts and, as far back as he could remember, Susan was a romantic and wanted reassurance that their love would last forever. Lying in bed with their arms around each other, she would ask him, "Will you always love me?"

And Sam would say, "Until the end of time."

Mickey remembered the first time Sam had shown him Susan's picture as if it was yesterday. It was indelibly inked in his mind not because she was a striking beauty, but ironically, because he found her to be so average looking. Sam had talked incessantly about how beautiful his wife was. Mickey had taken Sam's words at face value and constructed a mental picture of a woman of sufficient beauty to meet these unattainable expectations. When he saw the "real" Susan, he was understandably disappointed. She was a pleasant-looking woman but certainly not the knockout Sam had portrayed her out to be. He realized that Sam loved his wife so intensely that he saw her through a lens no one else could ever experience. He envied his friend's passion for his wife and wished he could someday experience this kind of overpowering love for a woman.

Medics removed his friend's body from his embrace, and a torrent of emotions overtook him. He grieved intensely for the loss of his friend and was awash in self-pity that he had never loved anyone as purely as Sam had loved his wife. He was consumed with guilt for feeling sorry for himself at a time like this and for being a survivor. Mickey sat down against the front tire of a wounded Jeep, pulled his legs up to his chest, put his head down on his knees and wept uncontrollably. Racked with grief, his body shook violently in spasms of unimaginable despair.

TWELVE

Mickey was suddenly aware that the hissing sound he heard was not steam coming from the cracked radiator of a Jeep from that earlier time but rather steam from a restaurant's industrial-sized dishwasher from the present. As he gradually became aware of his true surroundings, his eyes regained their focus and his first sight was the freaked out face of his fellow dishwasher. Biter's mug was only inches away from his.

When Mickey opened his eyes, Biter jumped up and hopped around, yelling, "Yes! Thank God! Oh, thank you, thank you, God! Thank you, thank you, thank you!"

To say Biter was relieved would have been an understatement. He feared he had driven Mickey over the edge and caused him to have a stroke or a heart attack. For all of Biter's faults, he wasn't a bad person and could never have lived with himself if he had been responsible for this man's demise.

"Oh Mickey, are you OK? What happened? I'm so very sorry. Please, please forgive me. I was just screwing around. I wasn't trying to hurt you."

Mickey pushed Biter away and stood up. "So, you just wanted to break my balls, and you didn't want to hurt me?"

"You know what I mean. I didn't want you to die or anything."

"But humiliating me was OK? What did I ever do to you? Why do you hate me so much?"

"I don't hate you," Biter said defensively. "We're just different that's all."

"Yeah, I know. You're the cool guy, and I'm the schmuck you like fucking with. Why do you have to put me down to puff yourself up? I don't understand it. You've got everything going for you. You're in good shape, you're not disfigured or ugly, and you're obviously smart. Only thing I can figure is that you were abused as a kid or something. Is that it? Cause then I could understand why you act like you do."

Biter was quiet for a long time. His silent shame was palpable. "No," he said. "I wasn't abused. I'm just stupid sometimes."

Mickey could sense Biter's remorse was genuine, but he wasn't ready to relieve him of his guilt just yet. It wasn't that he wanted to punish Biter for his actions. He just wanted to teach him a lesson, and he actually felt himself starting to like this guy that he used to think was a little prick.

"I suffer from PTSD. It stands for post-traumatic stress disorder. I experienced some pretty heinous shit when I was in Saudi Arabia during the Gulf War, and it fucked me up. I get flashbacks of the shit I went through when I'm stressed. My body can't take it, and I shut down.

Before I got sick, I wasn't much different from you. I was probably a little stuck on myself. I had a girlfriend. I had a lot of friends, actually, and was fun to be around. When I was on, I could charm the socks off people. But then I got fucked up by the war and lost all that. I wish I could go back, but I can't. You can't understand what it was like. You weren't there."

"I'm sorry, Mick," Biter interjected. "I didn't—"

Mickey broke him off. "I don't want your pity. I'm just trying to teach you something, so shut up. All I'm saying is that right now you've got the bull by the horns so enjoy it while you can, because you never know what lies ahead. Be thankful for what you've got now and show some charity to others that maybe aren't so fortunate."

Biter couldn't look at Mickey, so he stared at the floor. "I don't know what to say other than I'm sorry. I'd like to be friends."

Mickey extended his hand. "I accept your apology."

Biter grasped his hand like a drowning man. He couldn't think of anything to say that he felt was appropriate for the moment, but he couldn't let the silence continue. His mind searched for a fitting opening—something innocuous, something to lighten the mood, anything to transcend the awkwardness he felt at this moment. Even Biter was surprised by what came out of his mouth.

"You like the Stooges?"

"What?"

"You know, the Three Stooges."

Mickey started to laugh. "I did as a kid, but I haven't seen them in years."

"Me neither, but they're still funny, right?"

"Yeah, I guess so."

"Which one was your favorite?"

"Which of the Stooges? Oh, that's easy, Curly."

"Which Curly? Curly Howard or Curly Joe?"

"I don't know which one's which. I liked the first one, the original Curly."

"Me, too. Did you like Shemp?"

"Not particularly. Kind of hard to compete with Curly, don't you think?"

"I feel the same way. See, we do have something in common."

Mickey chuckled. "Yeah, I guess so."

Biter got a wild idea. He grabbed an unwashed aluminum foil pie pan and started to load it with food from other discarded plates from the dining room. He grabbed a few handfuls of turkey tetrazzini and mashed potatoes and threw on a couple of dessert cups of tapioca pudding. He handed the plate with the mound of mush to Mickey.

"Here. Pretend it's a pie. Throw it in my face."

Mickey started to laugh. "That's crazy."

"Come on, do it. It will be funny, and I deserve it."

"No. No way! It's stupid."

"Of course it's stupid! It's so stupid it's funny. That's the genius of the Stooges. Hit me with it!"

Mickey continued to laugh, but he couldn't bring himself to do it.

Biter knew he would have to provoke him. He searched the sea of rejected food on the dishes from the dining room and grabbed a piece of Devil's food cake off a nearby plate. As he shoved the cake in Mickey's face, he said, "Come on. It's easy. See?"

Without thinking, Mickey raised his hand and slammed the dish of slop into Biter's face.

The mushy concoction clung to his face like glue. Biter waited a moment for dramatic effect and then slowly raised his hands to wipe the food from his eyes. As he started to laugh, his potato-pudding-casserole face—with his beady, dark eyes and wide grin—looked to Mickey like a big smiley face. Mickey started to laugh uncontrollably.

Still laughing, Biter pulled an aluminum garbage can out from under the counter, hung his head over the can, and slowly scraped the slop from his face into the receptacle. When he had removed most of the food, he stepped forward and gave Mickey a big hug. As he started to release his grasp, Mickey tightened his and continued to embrace him for a while longer.

"See I told you it would be funny," Biter said, still laughing. "Come on, I guess we better start cleaning up this place. It's a real mess."

Biter knew someone would have to be held accountable for the broken dishes and glassware, so he wasn't surprised when he reported for work the next day and was immediately summoned to the restaurant manager's office.

The manager was a short, corpulent Jewish man named Zarenstein. When Biter had interviewed for the dishwasher position, he was impressed that Zarenstein had devoted a considerable amount of time, asking him about his background and why he wanted the job. He felt that the man actually took a personal interest in him and knew there were many other employers who wouldn't have given someone applying for this low-level position the time of day. He respected the man for the courtesy he had shown him and felt guilty that he had obviously let him down.

When Biter got to Zarenstein's office, Mickey was already in attendance, and he could see that he was extremely nervous. Biter took a seat next to him as Zarenstein began to speak.

"Oh, good, you're here. As I just told Mickey, I want an explanation for what went on in the dishroom last night. The amount of broken dishes and glassware is totally unacceptable."

Biter shook his head in agreement. "I can't agree more. It was totally my fault, and I take full responsibility for the damage. Mickey shouldn't even be in this meeting. I took my break at the worst possible time and left him alone. No one could have handled the dishroom all by himself at that time. It was poor judgment on my part. I should never have left."

Zarenstein looked confused. It was common knowledge that Biter and Mickey shared no love for each other, so he wasn't expecting him to come to his co-worker's defense. "So, you're saying, it was all your fault?"

"Absolutely," Biter answered.

"No, that's not totally true," Mickey objected.

Biter cut him off. "Yes it is. Mick is trying to cover for me, but I won't have him take the fall for my screw up."

Zarenstein raised his hands to stop any further discussion and shook his head. "Alright, I've heard enough. Mickey, you can go back to work."

Mickey stood up, looked Biter in the eyes, grabbed his forearm briefly and left without uttering a word.

Once he was gone, Zarenstein turned his attention back to Biter. "I know you are not being totally truthful with me."

Biter started to object, but Zarenstein cut him off. "Do you really think that I wouldn't have heard about Mickey inadvertently exposing himself in the dining room?"

"I didn't mention it because it had nothing to do with what happened in the dishroom afterwards."

Zarenstein smiled. "Let's be candid here. I know you were culpable in what transpired, but I also believe Mickey played a part in it as well. What I can't understand is why you are now taking full blame. It's common knowledge that you two don't get along, so I think you can understand my skepticism here."

"I've come to understand Mickey better recently," Biter offered.

"When you applied for this job, I knew from your academic background and work history that you wouldn't be here long, but you seemed like a hard-worker, and I had an opening I needed to fill. And you've done a good job up to now, but someone needs to be held accountable for the carnage in the dishroom last night. I'm sorry, but you leave me no choice. I have to let you go."

Biter extended his hand. "I understand completely."

Zarenstein was perplexed. He had fired numerous employees in the past, but no one had ever taken ownership for his own actions before, and he was impressed with Biter's veracity. He began to second-guess his decision but thought better of it and shook Biter's hand and asked, "No hard feelings?"

"None," Biter said truthfully.

As he turned to leave, Zarenstein added, "I still think there's more that you're not telling me, but I know this is the right decision. Good luck to you, son. I mean it."

THIRTEEN

When Biter returned home, he found JT sitting out on the deck feeding the Steller's jays. He gave JT a detailed account of what had transpired in the dishroom the day before and broke the bad news that he was once again out of a job. To Biter's relief, JT wasn't upset with him and actually seemed pleased that he had assumed the blame so Mickey could retain his job.

"That was pretty big of you, Biter," JT said. "I'm impressed."

"I guess I felt guilty for what I had done to Mickey by leaving him in the dishroom by himself. I didn't know he was going to freak out. If I had, I would never have done it."

"Maybe the lesson here is for you to learn to be less judgmental, especially toward those you don't hold in high regard."

Biter was obviously offended. "A minute ago you were giving me kudos for taking the fall so Mickey could keep his job. Now you are telling me that I'm an ass?"

"Biter, don't get me wrong. You are not a conceited person, and you generally have a big heart. So I find it strange that there are certain types of people you seem to have no respect for and show no charity towards. You certainly don't suffer fools easily, and you have no respect for people you see as weak, fat, or lazy."

Biter began to object, but JT once again stopped him. "Come on, be honest with yourself. I've heard you speak disdainfully about overweight people. For example, I've heard you say, 'This fat person did such and such.' My question is: Why was it important for you to mention that this person was overweight? I think the reason is that, in your mind, it's shorthand for saying the person is slow-witted, gluttonous or stupid. You'd get your back up if I accused you of being a racist, and I know you're not, but if you said, 'This black guy did this or that,' I'd say the same thing. Why was the fact that he was black worth mentioning at all? You wouldn't bother to mention that he was a white guy or that he seemed to be in good shape. You can protest all you want, but you know I'm right."

Biter looked away from JT and stared at the river. JT could tell his friend's feelings were hurt.

Biter suddenly got excited. "Look! There are three river otters swimming in front of your dock!"

Just as he said this, one of the otters disappeared below the water's surface. Within seconds, the water exploded, and JT and Biter could see that the otter had locked its jaws into a large salmon and the fish was struggling to free itself from the aquatic mammal's grasp. As the salmon thrashed around violently in a vain attempt to escape, the two other otters moved in and latched on to the fish to help their cohort subdue it. Working together, the three otters were eventually able to dispatch the fish and haul it up on the far bank where they began to feast on their quarry.

Biter was obviously excited. "Wow. That was pretty amazing!"

JT was equally stoked. "That's what I like about living on the river. There's something playing out in front of our eyes everyday."

Biter became quiet, and JT knew that he was still dwelling on their earlier conversation. He wanted to make sure his friend understood his criticism of him and knew that he valued his friendship. Although JT already knew the answer to the question he was about to ask, he pretended to be clueless to get Biter reengaged in their conversation. "Did you have river otters at the zoo you worked at?"

"Yes," Biter responded. "You saw them when I took you on a tour."

"Oh, there were so many animals, I forget. I bet the otters were a big hit with the public. You know, because they are so cute and cuddly."

Biter became animated. "Yeah, they are cute and appear playful, so the public naturally assumes they are warm and fuzzy, but they are still members of the weasel family and are voracious predators. If you stepped into their enclosure, they'd rip into your legs, and you'd quickly change your opinion of them."

That was the response JT was hoping for. "Exactly, looks are deceiving, and so are first impressions. That's all I was trying to get across to you earlier."

Biter looked intently at JT but said nothing.

"Biter, I think because you demand so much of yourself, you feel other people should meet the same standard, but everybody's different. Maybe if you learned to love yourself a little more, you might be able to lower the gauge by which you judge others."

Biter started to object, but JT cut him off. "Don't get me wrong, you are a loyal and honest friend and have a host of good qualities, but your experience with Mickey shows you that you still have things to learn in this life. We all do. I believe all the people we meet in our lives affect our spiritual development in some way. Maybe your experience with Mickey was meant to teach you that people are not defined by their physical appearances or mental capacities but by what resides in their hearts. Maybe this experience was meant to teach you to be more accepting of those you have habitually discounted in the past and to not be so quick to label those you really don't know."

FOURTEEN

JT worked as a bartender at a pub on the Newport Bayfront known as the Red Dragon. The establishment was owned by a sixty-something, half-crazed Korean woman named Mai. Although age and a hard life had weathered her appearance, the stresses of time and experience could not hide the fact that she was once a beautiful woman. When things were slow in the pub, JT would study her when she was unaware and try to imagine what her life had been like as a young woman. By the way she carried herself and dealt with men, he guessed that she, at one time, had either been a call girl or a madam.

She wore her hair pulled back severely in a bun and was always dressed in black. JT suspected her wardrobe choices were influenced by her movie selections. She spent her days in the bar, watching martial arts movies and westerns, while sipping on her never-ending rocks glass of bourbon, cracked ice and bitters.

The late afternoon crowd at the Red Dragon was an interesting mix of retired, old curmudgeons and middle-aged, alcoholic professionals, who showed up at the bar as soon as their workdays ended. The character of the place changed in the early evening as the retired folks went home to park themselves in their lazyboys and fall asleep in front of their televisions. A few of the functional drunks, who were not yet of retirement age, lingered until 10 or 11 p.m., but they were eventually replaced by the college students and yuppies, who then dominated the bar until closing.

Not surprisingly, Biter loved the place and fit right in. He frequented the pub whenever he came to visit JT and was on a first name basis with Mai and all of the regulars. The ringleader of the late afternoon contingent was Dylan Mackenzie, a rotund, black-haired lawyer in his mid-fifties with a thick Scottish brogue, who was better known by his nickname Mac.

As Biter entered the pub, he saw Mac sitting at the bar with two of his cohorts on his right—Will, a local fisherman, and Arnie, an elementary school janitor. A female, who looked like she was in her late forties and whom Biter had never seen before, sat to Mac's left. Although the woman was well-dressed, her platinum blond hair and heavy makeup gave her a cheap appearance. Biter had heard Mac speak frequently of his wife in deprecating terms, but he had never actually met the woman. He was curious to learn if this was, indeed, her and if she was as much of a harpy as Mac made her out to be.

Biter claimed the empty stool next to the woman as JT came to greet him from behind the bar and take his order. "Hey, cousin, what'll it be?"

"The usual."

JT turned to the beer taps and poured a barleywine for his friend. "I knew what your answer would be, but I still thought I'd ask," he said with a grin, as he placed the goblet on the bar in front of Biter.

Mac looked over to see who had sat down. "Oh! Hello, son. I didn't see you come in."

"Hi Mac. Are you going to introduce me to your friend?"

"Oh, excuse my poor manners. This lovely lady is… Oh, for fuck's sake, I already forgot your name."

"It's Lydia," the woman said, obviously irritated.

"Oh lass, there's no need to cop an attitude," Mac replied truthfully. "We just met, and I've had a few drinks, so I'm a might forgetful."

Lydia grabbed his hand and pulled it to her bosom as she looked intently in his eyes. "I guess I just thought that we were making a connection."

Mac pulled his hand away and said, "Well, as much as I am attracted to you, I can't lie to you, Lydia. I'm a happily married man. There's no chance of us shacking up tonight, so if that was your intention, you better look elsewhere."

"Who said anything about shacking up? So you think I'm a floozy?"

"No, I just know I'm cursed with good looks, and women all my life have had a hard time keeping their hands off me," Mac said in all seriousness.

Lydia jumped off her stool, grabbed her clutch purse off the bar and bolted out the door as Mac's drinking buddies roared with laughter.

Mac looked confused. "What's so funny?"

"Oh, Mac, you're a legend in your own mind," Arnie said predictably.

Biter knew better than to insert himself in the conversation, but he couldn't help himself. "Mac, I thought you'd jump at the chance to cheat on your missus. No offense, but you're always talking about what a witch your wife is."

"Well, that's a fact son, but if she ever found out that I had been unfaithful, she'd never let me hear the end of it. There'd be no escape from her constant harping, and she'd never agree to a divorce, even if I wanted one. She gets too much enjoyment out of making my life miserable. Why do you think I spend so much time here?"

"It's because you're an alcoholic," Will interjected. "Hey Biter, do you know why we call him Mac?"

"Yeah, it's short for his last name, Mackenzie, right?"

"No, it's an abbreviation of his nickname, MacLeod. I don't know who thought it up, but it's a reference to the fictional Scottish character, Connor MacLeod, in the movie, *Highlander*. Dylan's surname, Mackenzie, is a Highland Scottish name."

Biter couldn't resist having some fun with this news. "So Mac, you look young for your age. Wasn't Connor MacLeod, supposedly born sometime in the 16th century? That would make you, what? Almost 500 years old?"

"No," Will corrected him. "Mac just drinks so much, his liver feels like it's 500 years old!"

Again, his buddies roared with laughter.

Eager to have the focus of attention diverted elsewhere, Mac hollered at JT, who was waiting on another customer at the far end of the bar. "Son, I need a beer! I'm dying of thirst here. I feel like a camel in the Sahara!"

"I'll be there in a minute, Mac," JT responded. "I know you'll find this difficult to believe, but you're not the only person in this bar."

"No, only the most important," Mac retorted.

When JT was finished with his customer, he poured a pint of Mac's favorite, which was whatever happened to be the cheapest beer on tap at that time, and slid it across the bar to the Scotsman. "Here you go, Camel," JT said sarcastically.

Biter couldn't resist getting into the action. "I thought dromedaries had humps on their backs. It looks like gravity has taken its toll, and yours has slipped down to your gut."

Arnie pretended to make a jump shot. "He shoots. He scores!"

Will pressed his finger into Mac's arm and made a hissing sound like a match being lit. "H-s-s-s-s-s...BURN!"

Mac smiled broadly, but Biter could tell from the look in his eyes that he had gone over the line. He knew Mac had a reputation for playing practical jokes and guessed it would only be a matter of time before Mac found a way to pay him back for his smart-ass remark.

JT replenished Biter's drink and changed the subject. "Hey, Biter, I know you're looking for work, and we have an opening. You probably haven't heard, but Quinn, our relief bartender, was fired today. Mai caught him giving drinks to customers and pocketing the money. It's only part-time, but you like being the center of attention, and I think this would be the perfect temporary job for you while you look for something more in your field."

"Are you serious? I'd love it. Can you put in a good word for me?"

"I'll vouch for you, son, if you think that will help," Mac volunteered.

"Thanks, Mac, but I'd really like to get this job," Biter said in all seriousness.

JT laughed heartily. "Are you guys kidding me? We're talking about Mai here. There's no making any sense out of how she thinks. Biter, just go up and tell her you want to apply for the position. She'll either hire you on the spot or tell you to get lost. Either way, you'll have your answer in short order."

Biter looked over at Mai who was sitting on the customers' side of the bar by the grill, staring intently at the television screen. The movie she was watching was *The Good, the Bad, and the Ugly*.

Biter started to get off his stool before JT stopped him. "No, not yet. She's got a thing for Clint Eastwood. I'd wait until the movie is over before approaching her."

Biter nursed another drink and tried to anticipate what kinds of questions Mai might ask him. When the ending credits started to roll across the screen, he jumped off his stool and approached her. "Excuse me, Mai. Can I take a moment of your time?"

"Hello, Biter. What's on your mind?"

"JT tells me you're looking for a part-time bartender, and I'd like to apply for the position. I was hoping we could sit down and talk."

"Sure, take a stool," Mai said. "I've prepared some questions I was planning to ask potential candidates. I guess we can start with you. Would you like a drink?"

"Sure. I mean, is it OK, during an interview?"

"I'll be drinking, so I don't see why not. JT, give Biter another of whatever it is he is drinking on the house."

JT filled a goblet with barleywine and handed it to his friend with a wink. Mai rummaged through her purse, located her reading glasses and pulled out a bar napkin with writing on it. As she placed the glasses on her nose, she stared intently at the napkin. "OK, Biter, here's the first question. What's your quest?"

Biter thought this was a strange question to ask, but he knew Mai was Korean, so he chalked it up to a cultural difference and assumed she had merely chosen the wrong word. "Do you mean, what's my goal? I always thought I'd like to own a bar someday. Lord knows, I've frequented a few in my day, but I've never worked in one. I thought this would be a great opportunity for me to see if this is something I'm cut out for."

"OK, good answer," she said as she continued to study the napkin. Mai grabbed her rocks glass and took a healthy swig. After a long pause, she said, "Next question: What is your favorite color?"

"Red, but what relevance does that have?"

"I'm the one asking the questions," she barked. Again she raised her glass and took a drink and, again, she directed her attention to the napkin. "OK, next question: What is the air speed velocity of an unladen sparrow?"

Biter was confused and hesitated for a second, thinking that he had either misheard the question or that the barleywine he had consumed had taken its effect. Then it finally hit him. This was all a set up! He struggled to control himself and not show his hand. "English or African?" he asked, as a broad grin slowly consumed his face.

Mai couldn't help herself and started to laugh.

"Let me see that," Biter yelled, as he jumped up and wrestled the napkin out of Mai's hands and inspected it. "JT, this is your handwriting!" As he whirled around to confront his friend, JT and all of the regulars erupted in uncontrollable laughter.

"Screw you guys! My job interview is questions from *Monty Python and the Holy Grail*? Give me a break!"

Mai gave Biter a big hug. "The job was yours as soon as JT told me you'd be interested. All the customers like you. Just don't steal from me, and we'll get along fine. Can you start tomorrow?"

For a second, Biter was caught off guard and speechless. "Yes, of course," he laughed. "What time should I be here?"

Mai took a sip from her drink. "10 a.m. JT's already agreed to work the day shift tomorrow so he can train you."

"Thanks, Mai. And thank you too, JT, for going to bat for me, even if you are an ass!"

Again, the bar erupted in laughter.

FIFTEEN

The next morning, JT was all business as he showed Biter the ropes. "Look, I know you think this job is a piece of cake. It looks easy from the customers' side of the bar, but the fact is that it's more difficult than it looks. As a bartender you have to be all things to all people. There are times when you have to serve the role of someone's mother and provide a sympathetic shoulder to cry on. At other times, you're a father confessor for someone whose sins are too heavy a burden for him to bear alone. And there are still other times when you are compelled to be a policeman when some drunken SOB decides to get out of line."

"Wow, you're right," Biter agreed. "I never really thought about it, but I can think of instances where bartenders have served all of those functions for me and more over the years. One advantage I think I have is that I know a lot of the regulars here."

"Knowing their names is definitely a plus," JT concurred. "But now that you're a bartender, you are going to have to learn what they drink as well. The regulars expect you to know what they drink and how they want to be served. Let's take Mac, for example."

"He drinks the cheapest beer you have on tap," Biter volunteered.

JT laughed. "OK, that was probably too easy of an example. Let's take Arnie. What's his drink?"

"Gin and tonic?"

"Nope, vodka and tonic. What kind of service does he expect?"

"I guess I don't understand the question," Biter confessed.

"Knowing what a regular customer drinks is only part of the equation. You also need to know how he wants to be served. For example, if Arnie's glass is nearly empty, does he want you to bring him another vodka and tonic before he's done, or would he see this as presumptuous and want you to wait for him to order another drink first?"

"What difference does it make?"

"It makes all the difference in the world to these guys," JT explained. "Knowing what they drink and how they want it served makes them feel important, and it determines how big or small a tip they will leave you. Arnie wants there to be a new vodka and tonic on the bar when he finishes the one he is drinking. Will, on the other hand—who drinks Jack Daniels on the rocks, by the way—gets angry if you bring him another drink without checking with him first. Getting to know what they drink and how they want it served is key. Another thing you need to understand is that you are on probation."

"Of course," Biter said. "That's obvious. I have to prove myself to Mai."

"No. Mai only cares about the bottom line—how much money is in the till at the end of the day. You are on probation with our regulars. Like a fraternity, they have an initiation period for all newbies. You will not get a free pass because they know you or because we're friends. As I said before, you're on the other side of the bar now, and that changes everything. They will try to get your goat and push you to the limit because that's what they do with all new bartenders. They will try to make your life miserable to see how you react. It's their guilty pleasure, and they are not going to be deprived of it just because they like you."

JT then gave Biter a checklist of the opening and closing procedures and walked him through each item on the list so he could be sure Biter knew what was expected of him. When they were done, JT looked at the clock and saw it was nearly 11 a.m. "It's time to open for business," JT said. "Go unlock the front door and let Buzz in."

As soon as Biter turned the key, the door opened, and a stooped, little, elderly, white-haired man shuffled in. A widower, Buzz, had lost his wife of 56 years only nine months earlier. He was still grieving her death and struggling with his loneliness. Biter knew that he was always waiting at the door each morning when the bar opened, eager for the companionship of another individual, even if it was only the brief and sporadic company of his neighborhood bartender. He was always the first customer and, most days, the only patron in the pub for the first hour or so after opening.

JT felt sorry for the man and went out of his way to give Buzz as much of his time as possible in the morning on those days he worked the day shift. Biter watched how JT interacted with the old man and was both impressed with his ability to connect with Buzz and touched by his display of compassion. Biter could tell the old man loved recounting stories of his time with his wife, and he saw how skillfully JT drew him into conversation and then stepped back and listened intently as he let the old man verbally relive his cherished memories. As Buzz talked about his wife and their time together, Biter saw a transformation in the man. His lackluster, hazel eyes suddenly sparkled with renewed life, and his pallid complexion became ruddy. He seemed to forget his arthritic pain and become physically animated, moving about more freely as if he were a much younger man.

"My wife came to see me last night," Buzz said. "I wasn't dreaming. I was on the deck, looking up at the stars, and felt something lightly brush my forearm like a feather. I looked over, and she was standing next to me, smiling. She told me she was fine and that she loved me very much. She said it was time for me to end my grieving and get on with my life. She touched my hair, and I closed my eyes briefly, enjoying the moment. When I opened them again, she was gone."

"Did you actually hear her voice?"

"No…well, yes, in a way. Not with my ears, but in my mind. I heard her sweet voice and her gentle laugh, and there was no doubt in my mind that she was standing there next to me."

"I'm sure she was," JT said, struggling with all of his might to keep his composure.

Buzz looked up at JT with tears, welling in his eyes. "Do you think I'm crazy?"

JT smiled knowingly. "Buzz, you're not crazy. You're blessed. I have no doubt she'll be waiting to greet you when it's your time to cross over too."

Biter listened to this and was overcome with emotion. Tears started to stream down his face as he walked to the far side of the bar to compose himself. He looked back at JT and saw the old man, hugging his friend. Buzz wore a radiant smile on his face. JT excused himself and walked down the bar to Biter.

"JT, that was beautiful," Biter said. "You made Buzz incredibly happy. You are truly a good man."

JT stopped him. "Biter, before you give me too much credit, everything I said to him was true. I have no doubt in my mind that Buzz did see his wife last night. Other customers who have lost loved ones have told me similar stories. Their departed family member or friend either appeared to them or communicated with them in some way—either directly or through some meaningful symbol—a butterfly or a rainbow, for example, or through the presence of a characteristic smell, such as the aroma of the perfume or aftershave the loved one favored in life. At first, I just chalked it up to the hallucination of a grieving spouse or friend, who refused to accept the fact that his or her loved one was gone, but the stories sounded so similar that I felt there must be something to it. I went to our mutual friend, Pastor Doug, and recounted the stories and asked him if he had ever heard anything like this before. He laughed and said that he heard it all the time."

Biter had a myriad of questions he wanted to ask JT, but just then, the front door opened, and a group of four college students walked in the door. JT had Biter check their IDs before taking their order. After paying for two pitchers of beer, the students walked to the back of the bar and settled in at a table next to the pool tables.

"OK, Biter, time for your next lesson," JT said. "Let's pretend it's the evening, and this place is jumping with customers. You're here by yourself, and there's a group like these college kids who have been here for several hours drinking beer and playing pool. One of them comes up to the bar to get another pitcher. How do you know whether or not to continue to serve them?"

"I look at the guy's eyes and talk to him to be sure he's still sober."

"No, you have to have total bar awareness. The guy who is the least drunk is the one who is going to come up to the bar to get another pitcher. You need to tell the guy to go back to his table and that you'll come by in a minute to take their order. You want to check everyone out in their group before you give them another pitcher."

"Wow, there really is more to this than I thought. I'm glad I have a good teacher."

JT waved off the compliment. "Just don't let your friendship for a customer get in the way of your better judgment. Don't make exceptions for anybody. If someone is impaired, don't serve them, even if they say they are walking home or have a designated driver."

Will walked in and took his favorite stool at the end of the bar. Seeing him enter, Biter grabbed a rocks glass, filled it with ice cubes and then added a double shot of Jack Daniels. "Here you go, Will," he said, as he slid the glass across the bar.

"You know, Biter, Mac would probably hate me for telling you this, but by Mai hiring you, she has taken all of the fun out of us breaking in a new bartender. After you left the bar last night, we spent the better part of the evening trying to come up with a good way to give you shit, and we came up empty."

"Knowing you guys, I'm sure you'll come up with something," Biter replied.

The door opened, and Arnie waddled in and took his seat next to Will. As soon as he sat down, Biter had his drink of choice on the bar waiting for him.

"Looks like you're training him well, JT," Arnie said approvingly. "Can you pass me the remote?"

JT handed him the remote, and Arnie surfed through the channels until he located the Food Channel.

JT chuckled as he pulled Biter to the side and whispered, "You'd think they'd want ESPN or some other sports channel, but this is what these guys watch every day. They love watching some famous chef preparing a gourmet dish and then critiquing his creation. It cracks me up. Look at these guys. You know they don't know the first thing about fine cuisine."

Biter stifled a laugh. "Looks like today's featured entre is pork medallions. Let's see what our boys think of the chef's handiwork."

Arnie and Will sat quietly watching the TV and sipping their drinks. As the show progressed, Biter was struck by how little input they offered and said to JT, "Aside from the occasional approving grunt or 'Mmmm, that looks good,' they really offer no real insight."

JT laughed. "No, it's all about the end. Keep watching."

As the chef placed the pork medallions on the plate and arranged the broccoli, baby carrots, and orchid garnish around them, Arnie said, "It's all about the presentation."

Will concurred, "Yes, no question about it."

JT leaned over to Biter and said, "OK, here it is. Watch this."

As the cook poured the raisin-onion sauce over the pork, Arnie uttered a long drawn out groan, and Will added, "I agree. He just ruined it!"

"It would have been so much better with a truffle sauce," Arnie said, shaking his head in disgust.

"At the very least he should have added pignolias to the sauce he made," Will countered.

Biter turned to JT. "What are pignolias?"

"Pine nuts," JT whispered. Chuckling quietly, he grabbed Biter's arm and said, "These guys do the same thing every day. They watch the show and reserve their judgment until the end. It's always the cook's last move that ruins the meal."

"Looking at that food made me hungry," Will said. "JT, put in an order of gizzards for me."

JT struggled not to laugh. "Sure thing. Do you want anything, Arnie?"

Arnie scooped the last handful of complimentary pretzels out of the dish in front of him. "No, but I could use a refill on these."

JT whispered to Biter, facetiously, "I guess these guys are connoisseurs of fine cuisine after all." Looking up at the clock, he said, "Biter, it is 4 p.m. and time for you to fly solo for a while. I've got to go to the bank before it closes and run a few other errands. I won't be gone more than an hour or more, and this place shouldn't get busy until at least 6 or so. By then, Carl will be in to relieve us. Do you think you can handle it?"

"Piece of cake."

"Good. I'm out of here," JT said as he grabbed his jacket and headed for the door. Mac came in just as JT was leaving. "Where are you going, son? You're not leaving us here with this greenhorn are you?"

"Biter is more than capable. He shouldn't have any problems unless you guys create some. Be on your best behavior."

"Always, son, always," Mac replied as JT walked through the door. Mac mounted an empty stool, and Biter placed a pounder in front of him. "Here you go, Mac."

"Good job, son. I like the service. Keep that up, and we'll get along fine."

Checking to make sure Arnie's glass was still half full, Biter turned to Will. "Do you want another Jack?"

"Does a bear shit in the woods?"

Biter pretended to laugh at this lame response as he made him another drink. As he placed it on the bar, the front door opened, and a thin, slightly built man with tightly curled, brown hair and thick, black-rimmed glasses entered. Biter recognized the man as someone he encountered occasionally at his gym. Failing to remember the man's name, Biter resorted to a generic greeting, "Hey, friend, good to see you. What'll it be?"

"Well hello, Ray," the man said with a smile as he sat down immediately to Mac's left. "I'll have a lite beer, whatever you have on tap. I didn't know you work here."

"Just started today," Biter replied, as he poured the man a beer. "But I've been a customer here for quite some time, and I've never seen you here before."

"That's because I don't live nearby and only stop in on rare occasion. I'm a salesman and was just dropping off some product at a few of the gift shops on the Bayfront. It was the end of the day, so I thought I'd stop in for a quick one."

Biter smiled as he placed the beer on the bar. "Well, I'm glad you did. Good seeing you."

"Good seeing you too, Ray." Biter shook the man's hand and then directed his attention to his other customers.

Sitting next to the man, Mac couldn't help but hear the entire conversation. He was curious why Biter had not corrected the man when he had several times called him Ray, but Mac waited patiently for the man to down his beer and leave before confronting Biter. "Son, come here. I'm confused. Am I already drunk or did I hear correctly? Did the man who just left call you Ray? What's up with that?"

Biter laughed. "Oh, he's a guy I see occasionally at the gym. When we first met, he asked me what my name was, and I said Greg." Biter could see that Mac was confused. "Oh, that's right, you just know me by my nickname. My real name is Greg. Anyway, this guy mistakenly thought I had said Ray. I didn't bother to correct him, so he thinks my name is Ray."

"So why didn't you correct him?"

"Because he is only a passing acquaintance," Biter explained. "I rarely encounter him at the gym, and I really don't care what he calls me."

"So we can call you 'Shit' or 'Late for Dinner' and you'll answer to that?"

"As much as that would make your day, Mac, no way in hell!"

Mac laughed heartily. "OK, I was just checking." He dropped the subject, but was secretly thrilled that he now saw a way to haze the new bartender. He sat smugly on his stool drinking his beer and plotting his next move.

The front door swung open, and Carl, a short, muscular man with a shaved head, entered and took a stool on the customer's side of the bar. "Hey Biter, I see these yahoos haven't run you off yet, so I guess that's a good sign. Where's JT?"

"He went to run some errands. He should be back soon. Hey, thanks for changing shifts with JT so he could train me. I hope you don't feel slighted."

"Not in the least. You guys go way back, and it was fun to have the day off and enjoy the sun for a change. I don't get to work nights very often, and I'm assuming the night crowd tips better than these tight asses."

"You know we can hear you," Arnie said.

Carl looked pleased with himself. "So what's your point?"

"Looks like somebody just blew his tip," Will added.

Carl raised his eyes and pretended to be doing the math in his head. "Let's see, zero minus whatever is still zero." Hearing the front door open, he turned around and directed his attention to the entrance. "JT, you're back." Glancing down at his watch, he said, "And with just fifteen minutes left in your shift. Good timing as always."

"Hey Carl, thanks again for the shift change," JT replied, as he removed his jacket and reclaimed his position behind the bar. Biter excused himself. "I've had to go to the bathroom for an hour."

Mac waited for Biter to get out of earshot. "JT, I have a proposition for you. The boys have chosen a new nickname for Biter. If you agree to start calling him 'Ray,' we give you our word we won't do anything else to haze him."

"Ray? Where did that come from?"

"Look, we don't have a lot of time before Biter empties his tiny bladder. I'll explain it later. Suffice it to say, this is how we will initiate him into the brotherhood of Red Dragon bartenders."

Still confused, JT asked, "So what do I get out of this?"

"The satisfaction of knowing your buddy is getting off easy," Mac argued. "Remember how we hazed Carl?"

"They waited until I went into the can to take a piss," Carl volunteered. "And then they locked me in there for two hours until you came in to relieve me for the night shift. I still wonder how much we lost in free drinks that afternoon."

"Mac, you're lucky I never told Mai what you guys did," JT said. "I didn't say anything because I didn't want Carl to get into trouble. If it wasn't for that, you guys would have been 86'd."

"I thought the hundred bucks we anted up to keep you quiet took care of that."

Carl was incredulous. "They paid you a hundred bucks?"

"Oh yeah, I forgot," JT chuckled. "If I agree to call Biter by his new nickname in the pub, how long do I have to do this?"

"Until we get tired of it," Mac responded.

"So, in other words, for the whole time he works here?"

"Pretty much," Mac laughed with a pleased look on his face.

JT wanted more time to consider the offer, but Biter had just left the restroom and was headed back to the bar. "You'll be doing Biter a favor," Carl offered. "Give these guys enough time, and they'll think of something a lot worse."

JT was clearly uncomfortable about having to make this split second decision. "OK, I'll do it," JT said hesitantly. "Ray, get your jacket. It's six o'clock, and our shift's over."

Biter turned to JT with a confused look on his face. "Did you just call me Ray?"

"I'll meet you in the car," JT replied as he ignored Biter's question, grabbed his jacket and headed for the door.

SIXTEEN

Although Biter enjoyed bartending, he missed his job as a zookeeper and wanted to find work that would, at least in some way, utilize his training as a zoologist. Unfortunately, most job opportunities on the Central Oregon Coast were in fishing, logging or in the service industry, and there were few openings in anything even remotely connected to his former employment. To find something in his field, he knew he would realistically have to leave the area, but his heart told him that this was not an option. In the eight months that he had been living at JT's place, Biter had fallen in love with the area, and he knew that he belonged here.

It was not surprising then that when a part-time position for a research assistant came open at the local marine science center, he jumped at the chance to apply. Although you'd never know it by the way he acted most of the time, Biter had the ability to ingratiate himself with people and to make a good impression when he wanted to. The problem was that this was something Biter rarely wanted to do. However, since getting this job was important to him, he did his best to impress the interview panel and, as luck would have it, actually ended up securing the position.

Since it was only part-time, Biter knew that this job would not cover the cost of his monthly expenses and that he would have to continue to work at the bar to pay his bills. However, he hoped that this job would eventually lead to full-time work, and after a long stretch of what he perceived as bad luck, he was more than eager to believe that things were finally starting to go his way again.

The focus of his assigned research project was determining the growth rate of juvenile Pacific gaper clams in Yaquina Bay. Gaper clams are the largest clam species found in Oregon's estuaries and commonly grow up to five or six inches in length and can attain weights of two to three pounds or more. While Biter initially hoped that he would be conducting research on a species he considered sexy, like sharks or gray whales, he gained new respect for his research subjects as he learned about their life cycle during the first month of his employment. He also gradually warmed up to his assignment as he learned how to perform his research and operate the equipment he would be using in his work.

His mentor in this endeavor was Bailey Ford, a graduate student who was pursuing a PhD. in Malacology. Bailey was a tall, rather painfully skinny man in his early twenties with a thick mop of light blond dreadlocks and an unruly beard. He was incredibly smart and a computer geek, but he also loved to smoke weed and drink beer. Biter liked him immediately, and they became fast friends.

It was now mid-February, and the weather was unseasonably warm for this time of the year. Biter had lived in the Pacific Northwest long enough to know that this wasn't the advent of an early spring, but Mother Nature's way of being a tease. In his experience, there was always a stretch of five to seven days in February when the weather would be sunny and unusually warm. He also knew that it wouldn't last, and, just as suddenly as the warm weather had arrived, it would be gone, and they would be back to the cold realities of winter. Biter, however, loved the respite from the cold, wet weather and was more than willing to enjoy the sunny days while they lasted.

This was Biter's first day out of the lab and his first trip on the 20-foot research vessel he and Bailey would be using over the next few months to collect samples of clam larvae and newly set clams from predetermined subtidal sites in the bay. While it was Biter's first excursion, it wasn't Bailey's first trip of the year. He had been collecting samples of gaper clam larvae since January. However, the clams that had settled to the bottom were only now getting big enough to warrant Biter's inclusion in the research trips. When they got to their first station, they set anchor, and both men simultaneously went about their assigned duties.

Biter's job was to collect samples of the bottom, using a device known as a Peterson grab. It looked like the miniature bucket of a bulldozer, and he lowered it to the bottom of the bay from the side of the vessel with a winch. Its function was to collect a tenth of a square meter section of the substrate and all of the macroscopic organisms living in that slice of real estate.

While Biter lowered the grab to collect his sample, Bailey lowered a probe to collect temperature and salinity readings. He also employed a hydraulic pump to filter five cubic meters of seawater through a fine mesh net at both surface and near bottom locations to collect the plankton that was present at those depths in the water column.

As Biter retrieved the grab, he emptied the benthic sample into a plastic tub and then washed the contents through a series of 1-millimeter and 2-millimeter stainless steel screens. A variety of segmented marine worms, which biologists call polychaetes, writhed in obvious annoyance on the screens while a ragtag assortment of small crabs scurried frantically in all directions, searching futilely for some avenue of escape. Amid this riot of agitated invertebrates, Biter searched for the newly set gaper clams.

These young bivalves had abandoned their larval lives just weeks earlier to adopt a benthic existence on the sandy substrate from which they were now uprooted. Biter admired their Zen-like indifference as he watched them sit motionless in the screens with their shells shut, silently awaiting their fate. He wished he could confront the negative turns in his life with the same calm acceptance these clams now demonstrated, but he had to admit that his reaction to catastrophic events mirrored the more manic response of the polychaetes and crabs. Biter transferred the small clams to several plastic bottles, which he had filled with seawater from this site, labeled each with the station designation and then placed them in a plastic tub for return to the lab.

As Biter completed his work, Bailey rinsed the contents of his bottom plankton sample into a poly bottle, added buffered formalin to preserve the sample, and filled the remaining volume with seawater. He then recorded the station number and depth on the lid with a Magic Marker and placed it in a plastic tote. Turning to Biter, he said, "Did you say you have to work at the Red Dragon tonight?"

"Yeah, thanks for reminding me," Biter responded, with a disgusted look on his face.

"If I didn't know better, I'd think you hated working there. I've only been there a couple of times when you were on duty, but you seemed to be enjoying yourself."

"No, I usually like the job alright, but today is Taco Thursday."

Biter realized that Bailey didn't understand the significance of this. "The bar has daily food specials, and today is Taco Thursday," he explained. "The bar will be packed when I get there, and I'll be running my ass off most of the night. Thank God, I'm off tomorrow and won't have to work at either job. I won't have to see your ugly mug, and I won't have to put up with the regular customers at the Dragon either."

Bailey laughed. "I hear you talk about the locals like they make your life intolerable, but I've seen you interacting with them, and I'd have to say that you secretly care about each and every one of them."

Biter chuckled. "Am I that transparent?"

"Pretty much."

As Biter raised the anchor, Bailey started the engine, engaged the throttle and whisked them to their next station on their sampling transect across the bay. When they got to the site, the two men once again went about their business collecting their respective samples.

After they had completed their assigned tasks at this site, they allowed themselves a few minutes to engage in small talk before jetting off to their next station. They spent the next several hours following this routine. When they had collected their samples from their tenth and final station, they returned to the lab. As they unloaded their samples from the boat, Bailey said, "Well, we made good time and got back early. You should have more than enough time to tend to your new charges before heading off to the Dragon."

Once back at the lab, Biter transferred the clams from each of his samples to aquaria, which were continually fed with unfiltered seawater. On his next day at work, he knew his job would be to measure each clam to the nearest tenth of a millimeter. Those which were 4 millimeters or larger in length would be given an identifying number and marked with indelible red ink. The sorted clams would then be transferred to rectangular oyster trays, which were divided into multiple compartments lined with fine-meshed, plastic screening and filled with sand so that the clams had a substrate in which to burrow. Since the clams were filter feeders, he would then transport the trays to the dock outside their lab and suspend them from ropes a foot off the bottom. At this location, the clams would have access to plankton-rich bay water. He would then measure each clam on a weekly basis and record their shell lengths.

When Biter had taken care of his clams, he drove back to JT's place, made himself a sandwich and took a quick shower before heading to Newport for his shift at the Red Dragon. When he got to the bar, he pulled into the parking lot, but, as he expected, all the spaces were filled, and he was forced to park on the road a block away from the tavern and hike back to the bar.

As he opened the door, the assembled regulars, upon seeing him, predictably started singing, "TACO, TACO MAN" at the top of their lungs to the tune of the Village People's hit, "Macho Man." Biter smiled broadly as he crossed the threshold and made his way to the bar. He found it amusing that the regulars never seemed to get tired of this ritual and that this day's food special was responsible for him acquiring yet another nickname.

Although the beef and other ingredients that went into the tacos were prepared earlier in the day, it was Biter's job, in addition to tending bar, to assemble the ingredients and serve the tacos until all the meat was gone. He knew he was largely responsible for the popularity of this day's food special, and the irony of this did not escape him. When Mai decided to initiate Taco Thursday, he secretly made the decision to load hefty portions of fixings in each taco shell in an effort to get rid of it as soon as possible. In retrospect, he should have known he was creating a monster hit. At fifty cents a taco—especially ones that were loaded with the amount of meat he dispensed—this was an incredible deal, and the word traveled fast. The pub was always packed on Thursday nights at 6 p.m. when Biter came on duty and the special started.

Because of the size of the crowd that it drew and the volume of drinks that were sold, Mai decided to have the cook prepare as much taco fixings as her patrons could consume. Now, rather than getting rid of this inconvenience early in the evening as he had originally planned, Biter had to deal with it for at least half his shift.

Mai usually left the bar at about the time Biter came on duty, but the movie, *The Magnificent Seven*, had just started before he arrived. Biter knew she loved this western and the Japanese film that it was based on, *The Seven Samurai*, so he knew she wouldn't be leaving the pub anytime soon.

On other weekdays, the shifts of the day and night bartenders did not overlap, but on Thursdays, Biter needed time to dig himself out from under the initial avalanche of taco orders he typically was subjected to as soon as he arrived. Consequently, the daytime bartender Carl worked four hours overtime on Thursdays to give him time to do this.

As Biter washed his hands, Carl came over to greet him and give him an update of the day's happenings. "Hey, Taco Man, how are you doing?"

"Living the dream," Biter said testily. "I can't think of anything I'd rather do than dispense cheap food to the masses. I just wish Mai would give me a shovel rather than a serving spoon so I could complete the job in short order and be done with it."

Carl pretended to laugh, but Biter could tell that his reaction was not genuine for some reason. "We all have our crosses to bear," Carl said flatly.

"Is there anything I need to know about what went on today?"

"Oh, nothing out of the ordinary," Carl said. "Just that I'm on Mai's shit list again."

"Oh, what for this time?"

"Arnie won $500 on pull-tabs about an hour ago, and I was the one who reached into the bin and gave him the winning ticket."

"So you are in trouble for doing your job?"

"No, apparently I'm in trouble because Mai thinks I'm lucky and effectively serving the function of a rabbit's foot for the customers. I gave out a $250 winner to another customer earlier in the day, and this was the breaking point. Apparently, Mai thinks I have control over whether the tickets I pick are winners or not. She told me I was stabbing her in the back *and* giving away the farm."

"Well at least she made sure she wasn't missing any clichés in ripping you a new one."

Carl laughed reluctantly. "Yeah, you know Mai when she gets going. From the way she carried on, you would have thought I was just one step below Hitler on the heinous meter. I told her if I had a winning touch, I wouldn't be working for a crazy witch like her. I'd be in Vegas making bank and paying for high-priced call girls."

Biter's eyes widened noticeably. "Oh, that must have gone over big?"

"Yeah, I'm surprised I didn't get fired," Carl said. "So the end result is that I'm on probation for a month, and I'm no longer allowed to give pull-tabs to the customers."

"So who's supposed to do it while you're here tonight?"

"That would be you."

"So I have to be Taco Man and do pull-tabs too?"

"No. We're switching jobs tonight. Mai wants me to pass out the tacos until the orders die down to a manageable level and you are able to handle both jobs yourself."

"So you're Taco Man tonight?" Biter couldn't hide his elation. He grabbed Carl's head and planted a big kiss on his forehead. "That's fantastic! You *are* a lucky charm—you're *my* rabbit's foot!"

Carl pushed him away. "Biter, don't make me beat the crap out of you." He stormed off in a huff, then regained his composure and walked slowly over to the far side of the bar where the taco fixings were laid out. "OK, my friends," Carl yelled. "There's a new sheriff, I mean a new Taco Man in town. We're open for business."

Biter walked through the bar and checked with the customers at each table to see if anyone needed anything. Satisfied that he had the floor covered, he returned to the bar to assess the drink status of his regulars. He noticed that Arnie's drink was nearly empty and made him another vodka and tonic. Checking to make sure Mai was engrossed in her movie and not watching him, Biter slid the glass across the bar. "Here you go, Arnie. This one's on the house. It's a thank you for indirectly freeing me from Taco Man duty."

"Yeah, I knew you'd be pleased with the news," Arnie laughed. "But I feel bad for Carl. Mai came down on him pretty hard. She shouldn't have pull-tabs if she can't stand losing occasionally.

The house always wins in the long run, so I don't understand what she got so bent out of shape about."

"You're preaching to the choir," Biter said. "Where's your and Will's cohort?"

"Our what?"

"Where's Mac?"

"Oh, he had a friend coming in from back East, and he had to go to the airport to pick him up."

Biter looked surprised. "Are you kidding me? Mac's a lawyer. I didn't think he had any friends."

Arnie laughed. "Yeah, me neither. I guess it's a childhood friend. I've never met the man myself and neither has Will."

"I'm curious to see if you guys like him," Biter offered. "I used to think that my high school buddies would get along well with my friends from college because they both had something in common—they both had me as their friend. But I found that it never seemed to work that way.

This used to puzzle me, but then I realized that I had obviously changed in the intervening years and that the college Me was not the same as the high school Me. Since I had changed, my two groups of friends really had nothing in common after all. They each knew a different person, and so it really wasn't that surprising that they didn't hit it off. I also found that it made me feel awkward when the two groups met. I felt like I had to be the person each group expected me to be, and since I couldn't be both at the same time, I felt torn and really comfortable with neither."

"Well, we'll soon find out," Will said, as he stared out the window from his perch at the end of the bar. "Mac just pulled into the parking lot."

Within minutes the door opened, and Mac made his way to the bar accompanied by a distinguished looking man, sporting a Van Gogh-like beard and wearing an expensive Italian suit. The man had slate-gray hair, was tall and well built with one very noticeable exception—his arms were unusually short and disproportionately small in comparison to the rest of his body.

Mac and his friend claimed the stools next to Arnie and Will, and Mac made the obligatory introductions. "Hello gents, I'd like you to meet my very good friend, Rex. These are my bar mates, Arnie and Will, and our faithful bartender, Ray."

Biter could see that the man obviously had a birth defect but pretended not to notice. He knew he should extend his hand to welcome Mac's friend but was uncomfortable doing so. Instead, he just kept his hands behind the bar and smiled, broadly. "Welcome to the Red Dragon. It's a pleasure to meet you. What'll you have?"

"I'll have whatever Mac is having," Rex said.

Biter poured two beers and placed them on the bar. He then turned to Mac, leaned in close and said firmly under his breath, "Faithful bartender? I'm not Rin Tin Tin."

Mac laughed heartily. "Oh, Ray. It's so easy to get your goat. No reason to get offended. I was just pulling your chain." He paused briefly and chuckled, obviously pleased with himself. "And don't misconstrue my last statement. It wasn't meant as another dog reference."

Biter was angry with himself for taking the bait. He turned to Rex and said, "So I hear you and Mac go way back."

"That we do," Rex said. "We met the first day of class in Grade 3 and became fast friends." He then turned to face Mac. "We've had some good times in the intervening years, haven't we?"

"Oh, the best," Mac concurred. He looked at Biter and said, "Rex and I couldn't be any closer. We're the U.K. version of you and JT."

Biter looked surprised. "U.K.? Rex, don't tell me you're Scottish too?"

Rex chuckled. "Hell no, I'm English. That's what makes our friendship so remarkable!"

Mac laughed heartily. "Oh, for fuck's sake, it's getting deep in here." He then noticed that Will was staring noticeably at Rex's vestigial limbs, and he became visibly irritated. "Take a picture, it will last longer! Did your parents teach you no manners?"

Will feigned ignorance. "What did I do?"

Rex sensed Mac's embarrassment and patted him on the arm, knowingly. "OK, this is nothing new. Let's get this out of the way so we can have a good time and get drunk. Will, I know you've been staring at my arms and so has everyone else in this bar. It's something I've had to deal with all my life. It's a birth defect. I'm what is known in the medical literature as a thalidomide baby. Thalidomide was a drug some doctors prescribed to pregnant women in the late 1950s for morning sickness. I don't think it was ever approved for use in the States, but I'm living proof that it was used in the U.K. When a host of babies were born with severe birth defects like mine, scientists did further research and realized that this drug was the cause of their deformities. The use of the drug was eventually halted, but, by then, my script was written."

Biter saw that Rex's glass was nearly empty, so he gave him another beer. Feeling incredibly awkward and not knowing what else to do, he tried to apologize for Will's behavior.

"No apologies necessary," Rex said. "I actually think we are all being too hard on our friend, Will. He was just being genuine. Ray, when I walked up to the bar, you did your best to pretend that nothing was out of the ordinary, and I appreciate that, but your eyes betrayed your true reaction. They grew as big as saucers. And you didn't extend a hand in greeting. The only difference between you and Will is that you have a few more layers of subtlety and sophistication."

Biter didn't know how to react to this comment. "Thank you, I guess," he replied weakly.

"It wasn't meant as a compliment," Rex said candidly. "Ray, don't get me wrong. I know you did it with all good intentions. You didn't want me to feel awkward or different. But guess what? I am different. I'm used to people staring at me, and I'm used to the hurtful comments thoughtless people make. Let's get past that and get to know each other as friends."

Rex then turned to Will and looked him squarely in the eyes. "So in the spirit of full disclosure—in case you're wondering—other than my arms, everything else about me is normal." Struggling to keep a straight face, he added, "Well that's not totally true…there's one other thing about me that's different. There's an inverse relationship between the length of my arms and the size of my dick!"

Will looked puzzled.

Mac laughed heartily and nearly choked on his beer. "Will, it means that other than Rex's small arms and his huge willy, he's no different than you."

Biter was impressed with Rex's sense of humor. He knew he would never have the strength to handle such a heavy burden with the grace that this man showed, and it made him feel small. He struggled to keep his emotions in check, but couldn't control himself and blurted out, "I suck!"

Rex heard Biter's comment and was obviously confused. "Excuse me?"

Biter endeavored to explain. "You have such a great attitude that it makes me feel ashamed of how pathetically weak and superficial I can be. If I get a zit on my nose, I act like it's a big deal and want to hide. You've had to deal with major adversity in your life, and you handle it with dignity and humor. I wish I could have your strength and your outlook on life."

Rex smiled knowingly. "Before you get too down on yourself, Ray, let me make the point that I was born this way. I've never known anything different, and I've had a long time to come to terms with my situation. I wasn't always comfortable in my own skin. If the truth be known, my friend Mac here had a lot to do with me accepting who I am.

I know I don't have to tell you that little kids can be cruel. When Mac and I were growing up, the kids in the neighborhood used to mock me unmercifully. I was always big for my age and towered above the other boys so you'd think they wouldn't mess with me, but because I had small arms, I was viewed as a freak and considered fair game. I don't know who came up with the nickname, but nearly everyone in school started calling me *T. rex*, which was an obvious reference to the dinosaur, *Tyrannosaurus rex*.

At first, I hated the name because it was intended as a term of derision, but Mac encouraged me to embrace it. I can recall one time—when I was especially down on myself—that he grabbed me by my shoulders and shouted, 'Hey, dinosaurs are cool. Which one was the biggest, baddest dinosaur of them all? It was *T. rex*! And who's my biggest, baddest friend of all time? It's you! From now on, I'm calling you Rex!'

We were just kids, so I'm sure Mac didn't realize at the time just how profound his advice really was. But it was brilliant! Words only have the power that you give them. When my friends and I embraced my nickname, it ceased to be a weapon for the bullies, and they stopped taunting me."

Mac laughed. "Rex is being too modest. The reason he stopped being harassed was because he turned out to be an awesome soccer player in high school and was responsible for us winning the championship game. He was a hero, and everyone loved him. I just hung around him to have a chance with the birds that he attracted."

Rex roared, "Oh that's rich. Ray, don't believe a thing he says. He's a lawyer, don't you know?"

Biter didn't know who to believe, but he was impressed with the strong bond the two men obviously shared and enjoyed their friendly banter. As he thought about the many good-natured, verbal fencing matches he and JT had engaged in at this very bar, a long smile crept slowly across his face. He was impressed that Mac had seen a parallel between his friendship with Rex and his own with JT. He made a mental note that he might want to reconsider his opinion of Mac. He had always known that the guy was smart, but he now appreciated the fact that the man was a lot more complex than he had previously given him credit for.

Halfway down the bar, a patron, who was waiting to be served, couldn't contain himself any longer. In a thick and obviously fake Scottish accent he yelled, "Bartender, I'm dyin' of thirst here! I feel like a camel in the Sahara!"

Even with the accent, Biter, Mac and his barmates recognized the voice immediately and erupted in a fit of laughter. It was JT!

Biter ran down the bar and asked sheepishly, "When did you get here? I didn't see you come in!"

JT just shook his head slowly in mock disgust. "So this is total bar awareness? Is this what I taught you?"

Biter was obviously embarrassed. "I'm usually really good about that, but Mac brought in his friend Rex, and I lost my focus."

JT laughed. "I'm only giving you shit. The parking lot was full as it always is on Thursday nights. I had to park on the street a block away and came through the door in Mai's office. I saw you were engrossed in conversation with the boys so I thought I'd bust your chops."

Biter relaxed, filled a glass with beer and slid it across the bar to JT. "I should have known. When will I ever learn?"

"Hopefully never," JT replied. "It's too much fun getting your goat!"

"So I hear," Biter chuckled. "So I hear."

The problem with Mai lingering past 6 p.m. was that she didn't alter her drinking habits to account for her extended stay. She made sure her rocks glass was always full and just got more and more inebriated as the night went on. Unfortunately, alcohol did not bring out the best in her. As Mai's level of intoxication grew, so did her propensity for argument.

If there was a chance of her getting in her car and driving, Biter would have had good reason to refuse to serve her, but she had given her keys to Carl as soon as she realized she wouldn't be leaving at 6 p.m. as usual. She gave him explicit instructions that she, under no circumstances, was to be given them back until the next morning. Biter knew she would end up sleeping on the couch in her office, as she had done many times before. Still, for Mai's own well-being and for Carl, who would have to put up with her in the morning, he was anxious to lessen her alcohol intake as much as possible. He went to JT who was still sitting at the bar to ask his advice.

"Is there anything I can do to stop Mai from getting as drunk as she would otherwise?"

JT smiled, obviously enjoying the moment. "Oh Grasshopper, listen and learn. Fill her glass with cracked ice and bitters and only float a small amount of bourbon on the very top so that—when she takes her first sip—she tastes the alcohol and thinks it's a stiff drink."

"Will that work?"

JT looked over at Mai and studied her for a minute. "Oh yeah, she's definitely drunk enough. She'll never notice." He then downed the last of his beer and handed the empty glass to his friend.

Biter retrieved a new mug and filled it with JT's favorite beer. Handing it to his friend, he said, "I knew you'd have the answer."

JT replied, "You know, it's not rocket science. You pick up these tricks when you've done the job as long as I have. I'm just happy to help."

For the next few hours, Biter consumed his time, keeping the glasses of his cadre of customers filled with their favorite libations. During that time, Biter continued to water down Mai's drinks, and, to his relief, she was none the wiser. Once the taco fixings were gone and the crowd started to thin out, Carl left for the evening, leaving JT and the regulars to keep Biter company.

When there were only twenty or so customers left in the bar, Biter approached Mai and said, "It's been a long day. I'm surprised you haven't retired for the evening."

"Oh, I've been killing time waiting for my next movie. *Rio Bravo* is scheduled to start in five minutes."

Biter had seen the movie years ago and knew it was a John Wayne film. "I know you like the Duke. Is this one of your favorites?"

"I love *Rio Bravo* because it also has Ricky Nelson. I had a crush on him when I was a teenager. He was so hot! If I had ever gotten to meet that 'Travelin Man,' he would have settled down, if you know what I mean. Why search the world for chop meat when you can have filet mignon at home?" Mai was obviously pleased with herself, and she giggled like a young girl. Biter found this endearing, and it made him even more curious to learn more about her history.

Mai suddenly turned serious. "Do you see the two men who are playing pool directly behind where I'm sitting?"

Biter surveyed the two males. Both were middle-aged. One was tall, slender in build and balding. The other was considerably shorter but was swarthy in appearance and had thick, black hair, which he sported in a rockabilly hairstyle. "Yeah, I see Mutt and Jeff, so what?"

"They are both with that one woman who is sitting at that table directly behind the pool table."

Biter then directed his attention to a rather plain-looking woman who he guessed was in her mid-forties. She had tight, curly, salt-and-pepper hair and piercing green eyes.

Mai continued. "The two men have been arguing amongst themselves for most of the time that they've been here. At times, I could hardly hear my movie. The tall man is that woman's husband. The shorter one is her new lover. They're swingers. From what I could gather, the new guy doesn't want the husband to watch or participate. The husband is all pissed off, and the two men have been going at it pretty good. It's all been just bluster so far, but I want you to be aware of the situation in case a fight breaks out. I'm not worried. JT is still here, and I know you and he can kick their asses if it comes to that."

"Thanks for the confidence and the heads up, Mai."

Biter walked over to JT and related to him what Mai had said.

"Wow, the old girl is still pretty sharp," JT said. "I've been watching them myself and was waiting for the right time to say something to you. She's spot on. The new guy doesn't want the husband to play, and that's the source of their argument."

"Should I kick them out?"

"For what, for being kinky? I think that's their business, and it's getting pretty late. Hopefully, they'll leave soon, and we won't have to get involved."

Biter went about his business but kept a watchful eye on their actions. To his dismay, the two men continued to play pool and continued their constant bickering.

As his wife's new boyfriend looked down his pool cue, eyeing his shot, the husband said in frustration, "You knew the rules when you answered our ad. You had no problem with it in the beginning. Why now?"

The shorter man hit the cue ball with too much force, and the targeted ball ricocheted off the pocket and failed to go in. "Because, it's getting old. Your wife is in love with me. I satisfy her, which you apparently never could. You're like a third wheel on a bicycle. You really have no function, and we don't want you involved any longer in our relationship."

The taller man was visibly upset and turned to his wife. "That's not true. Tell him that's not true."

The woman looked down at the table and quietly uttered, "Let's be honest, you and I haven't been intimate for a while now. I think that's why we resorted to this. We both wanted something else. It was OK in the beginning, but I want a normal relationship now."

The husband became enraged. "You two-timing slut! You think you're some kind of prize? Look in the mirror. You're overweight and showing your age. You're lucky you married me!"

Mai wanted to enjoy her movie, but the invective had risen to a new level, and it was impossible for her to hear the dialog. Dean Martin in *Rio Bravo* had just started singing, "My Rifle, My Pony and Me," and when Ricky Nelson joined in to accompany him and Mai couldn't hear his voice, she became incensed. She jumped off her stool and wheeled around, confronting the two men. "Shut up! Shut up or fight! I'm sick of hearing your crap. Come on pussies, fight! Fight!"

Her words obviously galvanized the two men to action. The husband swung his cue stick back and forth like a sword, trying to hit his rival in the gut. His wife's new lover instinctively jumped back from the table, and when he saw an opening, he lunged forward, grabbed a pool ball, and threw it at his rival. Although it missed its mark, it was the spark that Biter and JT had dreaded.

The two men started lobbing pool balls wildly across the table at each other. The balls came raining down on nearby tables and on the bar itself. One nearly hit Mac and Rex as it sailed past their heads and hit the mirror behind the bar directly in front of them, shattering it. Another came crashing down on a table in the back of the bar, sending shards of glass and alcohol in all directions. The handful of people who were still in the bar took cover under their tables. Biter, who was taking drink orders on the floor when the fight erupted, dove beneath the nearest pool table to escape the rain of cellulose hailstones. JT jumped off his stool at the bar and joined his friend on the floor under the table.

When the two foes ran out of ammunition and their rain of pool balls subsided, JT turned to Biter and said, "I'm tired of these creeps! It's time to kick some ass." He rolled out from under the table, jumped up and tackled the husband. As the man struggled to turn around and fight back, JT gave him a roundhouse right and broke the man's nose.

As the man's proboscis bled profusely, JT stood over him and threw him a wad of napkins from a nearby table. "Here, use these and put some pressure on the base of your nose to stop the bleeding. If you even think about getting up off the floor, I'll knock you senseless."

Seeing this, the boyfriend started to run for the door and said, "I'm going to get my gun."

Biter reached out and grabbed the man's leg as he ran past his pool table. As the man came crashing to the floor, Biter jumped up and grabbed the man around the neck and put him in a headlock. As the man struggled to get free, Biter tightened his grip and cut off the man's air supply. As the man slowly fell limp in Biter's arms, he relaxed his hold to give the man some air. To his surprise, when he did this, the man rose up and continued his flight for the entrance. Biter jumped up and got to the door just as the man was opening it. He slammed the door shut and said, "You son of a bitch, you're not going anywhere." The man then veered left and ran toward the bar in an effort to get away from Biter, but Rex hopped off his stool and blocked the man's exit. As the man paused to decide which way to run, Rex planted a perfect kick to the man's groin, and he fell to the floor, writhing in pain.

Biter walked over to the man, looked down at him and said, "You broke a mirror. It looks like your seven years of bad luck has just started." Biter then turned to Rex and patted him on the shoulder. "So you *are* a soccer player. That was an impressive kick. I can't believe you could hit a target that small."

Rex just smiled.

Just then, Mai emerged from her office with a 12-gauge shotgun and confronted the threesome. "OK, this is how it is. Nobody breaks up my bar. This is my family. I've survived two wars and three abusive husbands. I'll be damned if I'll let some freakshows like you ruin my business. I'm calling the cops, and you are going nowhere until they get here."

Mac calmly got off his stool, took one last swig of beer and then cleared his throat. "Mai, I couldn't agree with you more. We are just one big family here, and we don't need strangers like this coming into our bar and causing a ruckus. But I think JT and Ray have everything under control, and I don't think you really want to call in the cops. If you do, they'll be breathing down your neck for months after this, and it will hurt your business. Let me see if I can work out an accommodation where all parties will be happy."

The woman who was part of the threesome was nearly hysterical. "I agree. We don't want any trouble."

Mai lowered her shotgun and turned to Mac. "You're my lawyer. I trust you. I'll leave it up to you. I'm going to bed." She walked behind the bar, and as she made her way to her office, Biter could hear her singing, "My Rifle, My Pony and Me." He turned to JT and said, "She sounds like Joe Cocker." JT and the other regulars who heard his comment broke up laughing.

Mac fought back a smile but stayed focused, looked at the woman and said, "You have two choices here. We can call the cops, and you and your friends can give them your version of events. But we will still take you to court to recover damages, and we will expose your lifestyle in the process. I trust you'd like to avoid that embarrassment. The other alternative is for you to pay for the damages right now. It is totally up to you. It's your choice, and I want you to understand you are under no duress to choose one alternative over the other. You have my word we will abide by whatever decision you make."

The woman was shaking noticeably and said, "I've made up my mind. Please don't call the cops. I'll give you my credit card, and you can charge whatever you think is fair."

Mac looked at the handful of people who were still in the bar and recognized most of them as regulars. "Was anyone hurt here?"

Everyone shook their heads in the negative.

Mac turned to the woman and said, "Well you are really fortunate. I'd say you could make this problem go away for a mere $2,000. A court case would be embarrassing and certainly cost you a lot more."

The woman grabbed a credit card from the wallet in her purse and said, "Done."

Biter ran the card, and when the transaction was completed, he returned the card to the woman and gave Mac the go-ahead to let the threesome leave.

The two men were then allowed to struggle to their feet and limp out of the bar with the woman. As the three of them left the bar, JT said, "I don't think any of them are in any condition to get their freak on tonight." He then patted Mac on the back and said, "Good job. How did you arrive at a figure of $2K?"

Mac chuckled. "I guessed that the mirror will cost about a thousand bucks to replace, and Arnie told me Mai lost $750 in pull-tabs today. I figured that left about $250 in free drinks to compensate those of us who were in the bar when this traumatic event transpired. I know I'll have difficulty sleeping tonight, and it might go on for several weeks. Ray, I want to start claiming what my friends and I are due. I'd like free beers all around, if you don't mind."

Biter laughed. "I don't think that will be a problem." He walked behind the bar and started filling pint glasses with beer.

JT chimed in, "Ray, include me in that as well. I'm so traumatized, I don't know if I'll be able to report for work tomorrow evening. You better make my drink a barleywine."

Biter just shook his head. "Yeah, whatever. You guys just better drink up. It will be last call in about a half an hour, and after I close and clean up the place, it will be my turn to self medicate."

SEVENTEEN

The western pond turtle's painfully slow progress across the two-lane road reminded Biter of himself as he typically hobbled to the bathroom in the morning to relieve his bladder. Arthritis seemed to run in his family, and he noticed that his joints were beginning to give him some discomfort even at this early age. It was especially noticeable on a cold, late winter morning like this. What a depressing way to begin the day, he thought, as he sat in his truck, rubbing his cold, aching hands. Once the shelled reptile had safely disappeared in the marsh grass on the far side of the road, he depressed the accelerator and traveled the remaining half mile to his destination. He pulled his truck over to the shoulder and exited the vehicle.

Trading his shoes for the hip waders on the floor of the passenger's side of the cab, he walked to the back of the vehicle and grabbed the shovel and white plastic bucket that were in the bed of his truck. After checking to make sure that his rubber gloves and vernier calipers (his clam measuring device) were still inside the five-gallon container, he patted the breast pocket of his jacket to make sure his mechanical pencil and Rite in the Rain notebook were contained within it and then headed out across the marsh. His destination was the far tip of land that jutted out into the bay just before it emptied into the ocean. This was where he had planted his juvenile clams. For nearly seven months, he had raised these diminutive bivalves in oyster trays he had suspended from the dock outside the marine lab. He had moved his clams to this new location on the marsh in late September so their survival would not be threatened in the winter months when they would inevitably be exposed for an extended period of time to cold air temperatures during low tides.

However, like almost everything else in life, the marsh location had its pluses and minuses. At their new location, the clams would have a much better chance of surviving the winter, but they would also be more likely to escape confinement and be accessible to scrutiny only briefly during the most extreme low tides, twice a month.

Unlike barnacles and oysters, which cement themselves to the substrate at the end of their planktonic existence, young gaper clams burrow shallowly into the sand and can be dislodged by strong tidal currents. To keep his clams from traveling across the beach, Biter had created a mini-corral by driving four metal posts into the ground, trenching in small-meshed plastic netting about six inches into the sand around the perimeter and then securing it to the uprights about a foot above the substrate.

Biter could see that the outgoing tide was now in full retreat, and he hurriedly made his way across the marsh to give himself as much time as possible to locate and measure his clams. From his earlier trips, he knew that a straight-line trajectory to his destination was not possible. There was a creek directly in front of him, which was too wide and too deep to forge. To get across it, he had to travel eastward for some distance through a thicket of willow and alders until he found a place where the creek was narrow enough for him to jump across.

Once across the channel, he weaved his way through the labyrinth of reeds and small ponds that dotted the landscape until he came to the outermost point on the marsh. His timing was nearly perfect, for his clam containment pen was just beginning to become exposed as he arrived at the site. Biter was pleased to see that the pen had weathered the tides well and was only in need of slight repair.

He planted his shovel triumphantly in the sand as if planting a flag on hard-won territory. The purpose of the shovel was not to unearth his clams, for the shells of his research subjects were still too thin and delicate for this. Rather, the digging utensil was to be used as needed, to re-trench the netting that had been dislodged by the currents since his last visit.

Biter had to locate his clams by searching blindly in the substrate with his hands, the way a raccoon uses its tactile sense to find food in the shallows of a lake or pond. He needed the rubber gloves he had brought along to prevent his fingers from becoming lacerated by the broken razor clam shells that were scattered in the sand. Shards of these shells were paper-thin and as sharp as a straight razor—the barber's tool these bivalves resembled in shape and from which they derived their common name.

Biter donned his rubber gloves, knelt down next to the pen, plunged his hands slowly into the sand and began searching gently for his diminutive charges. In less than a minute his index and middle fingers detected something solid in the substrate, and he retrieved his first clam. He rinsed off the sand from its shell in the shallow water, examined the clam's condition, and recorded the identifying number, which was indelibly marked in red ink on its shell, in his notebook. He used his calipers to measure the bivalve's length, recorded this data and then placed the clam in his bucket for temporary holding while he searched for its cohorts.

EIGHTEEN

To the tow-headed, ten-year-old, the marsh was a wondrous world of creepy crawlers and the perfect springboard for an unforgettable flight of fantasy. As the boy made his way across the wetlands, he unwittingly spooked a great blue heron, which was standing motionless in the shallows in search of prey. As the bird took flight, it uttered its characteristic, guttural croak. Upon hearing this grating vocalization, the youth instinctively ducked his head below the surrounding cattails and imagined the source of the sound to be a prehistoric pterodactyl.

The boy loved the excitement and perceived danger of the marsh. Living nearby, he visited the site as often as he could, and each excursion offered the promise of a new adventure. One day, he might be an African explorer, setting out into the "Heart of Darkness." The next, he might be an astronaut, visiting Mars and searching for little green men. The beauty of being ten was that his marsh world was only limited by the extent of his fertile imagination.

Today's outing was as yet unthemed as the boy busied himself with one of his favorite pastimes—searching for salamanders and other amphibians. That was before he caught his first glimpse of a man on the outer reaches of the marsh, digging in the intertidal. The boy was accustomed to having the wetlands as his solitary playground, and the sight of another person out there intrigued him. Being rather timid, his tendency was to avoid contact with strangers, but his curiosity got the best of him, and he had no choice but to find out what this man was up to. To do so without being detected required stealth, and he was eager for the challenge. He pretended to be a soldier, performing reconnaissance behind enemy lines. His job, as he imagined it, was to infiltrate the enemy's camp and obtain critical information on his subject's activities.

The boy crouched low and began to creep toward the stranger using the tussocks of cordgrass that dotted the landscape as cover. As he made his approach, he encountered a muddy slough, which was impassable, and he was forced to skirt along the edge of the channel as it wound its way to the beach. Following this circuitous route, he eventually came to the edge of the marsh, ending up about fifty yards north of the stranger's position.

The boy slowly poked his head out through the reeds and peered across the marsh. The man, who was still some distance away, was clad in a red and black plaid wool jacket and waders. He was on his knees in a few inches of water, bent over and engaged in some activity. However, since the stranger's back was turned to him, the boy couldn't see the man's face or determine exactly what it was that he was doing.

The boy wanted to get a better view of the man and decided to abandon the safety of the marsh grass and sneak a little closer. He got down on his stomach and began to crawl toward a pile of driftwood that was stranded on the upper reaches of the shore a short distance in front of him. As he inched his way closer to a large log on the edge of the pile, the timber not only hid his presence but also blocked his view of the stranger. Upon reaching the driftwood, he raised himself up on his forearms to see over the obstruction. Lying in the depression on the other side of the log, just a few feet away, was the body of a dead man!

The boy gasped in horror and jumped back, falling face down in the sand. He tried to remain motionless, but his adrenaline rush won out, and his body shook noticeably. With the sound of his heart pounding loudly in his ears, he used his arms to slowly raise himself up off the sand and peeked over the log. To his relief, the stranger was still at work in the shallows, so he knew that he had not given himself away. He stared down at the badly decomposed body. The dead man was dressed in a pair of black trousers, but his feet were bare, and he was naked from the waist up. Only a thin veneer of skin still covered the man's torso, and his ribs were clearly visible beneath this shroud of tissue. To the boy, it was as if he had X-ray vision, and he found the view to be both oddly sickening and fascinating at the same time.

The boy turned his attention back to the stranger and saw that the man was now upright and digging in the sand with his shovel. He guessed that the man was excavating a grave in which to bury the body, and he wanted to get away before the man came toward him to retrieve the corpse. He got back down on his belly, turned around and crawled briskly back to the cover of the marsh grass. Checking one last time to be sure that the stranger was still unaware of his presence, he hopped up on his feet and ran frantically across the marsh, dodging potholes and cattails with abandon. He never looked back and didn't stop running until he was home.

NINETEEN

Biter ran his gloved hands through the sand one last time in a vain attempt to find his last remaining clam. Time was running out. The incoming tide was starting to cover his mini-corral and was now rushing in at a rapid pace. He knew he could wait no longer and emptied the clams he had recovered back into their containment pen. He placed his mechanical pencil and notebook in his breast pocket and slid the vernier calipers into the right hip pocket of his wool jacket. He then spent his remaining minutes re-trenching the perimeter netting.

Satisfied that his clam containment pen was as secure as he could make it, Biter removed his rubber gloves and placed them in the bucket, grabbed the rest of his gear and headed off the marsh. As he made his way across the wetlands, he noticed a sheriff's car, barreling down the highway with its lights flashing but its siren silent. He visually followed its progress and was surprised to see the vehicle slow down and pull immediately behind his truck on the edge of the road. Just as the officer was getting out of his car, Biter came to the same creek that had blocked his passage earlier, and he was once again forced to move inland through the thicket of willows and alders to find a fordable point to cross the water hazard.

Crawling Back To Start

To the deputy sheriff watching his movements, Biter's detour through the trees looked suspiciously like an attempt to avoid capture, and it reinforced his preconceived notion that the man on the marsh was a murderer. The tall, lanky officer took up a position far enough away from the trees where he would be able to see the suspect clearly as he came into the open. As Biter exited the trees, the officer ran up to confront him, drew his gun and yelled, "Freeze!"

Biter understandably was unnerved by the sight of a gun barrel staring him in the face, and he became nearly apoplectic with rage. "Are you crazy? What's going on?"

The young lawman ignored his questions and barked, "Show me your hands!"

Biter quickly dropped the shovel in his left hand, but for some inexplicable reason, held onto the plastic bucket with his right as he raised both arms above his head. He could see that the officer was about his age and that this man was as uncomfortable with the situation he found himself in as he was. Biter guessed that in a lazy, coastal town like this a policeman saw little action and was accustomed to writing speeding tickets for the tourists, making DUII arrests, and breaking up marital disputes between the locals. "Calm down," Biter said nervously. "I don't know what crime you think I've committed, but I've done nothing wrong."

The officer extended his gun hand ever so slightly to indicate that he meant business. "What are you doing out here?"

"I was measuring my clams."

The officer was incredulous. "Your what?"

"Clams," Biter said.

"Are you kidding me? Where are they? Show them to me!"

"I can't," Biter said truthfully. "I put them back."

"Put them back? Do you think I'm a total idiot? What's in the bucket?"

Biter started to lower his right arm to show the officer the contents of his bucket. As he did so, the young lawman became nervous and screamed, "Put your hands up!"

Biter quickly raised his right arm but yelled in obvious frustration, "You asked me what was in my bucket! Make up your mind!"

The officer countered, "Keep your hands up and drop the bucket!"

Biter complied, and the bottom of the bucket hit the muddy dirt with a hollow thud, releasing its contents as it fell on its side. The officer stole a glance at the ground and saw a lonely pair of latex gloves, extending like two multi-forked tongues from the mouth of the container. He quickly returned his full attention to the suspect. "Sir, what is the purpose of the latex gloves?"

"I need them for recovering my clams."

"Isn't that what the shovel is for?"

"No. The clams are too small for that. I need the shovel to repair the corral I keep them in," Biter explained.

The deputy was clearly frustrated. "Are you on drugs? Your answers make no sense. I'm going to ask you one last time, and if you can't or won't provide a credible explanation for your presence on the marsh, you leave me no choice but to take you into custody for further questioning. Now, what were you doing out there on the marsh?"

"I'm telling you the truth. I'm a research assistant at the marine lab. I work for Dr. Husker. He's studying the growth rate of gaper clams. Look, I have his business card."

As Biter began to lower his right arm to retrieve the card from his wallet, the deputy became unhinged. "Raise your right arm now! I didn't give you permission to move!"

"I was just going to—"

The deputy cut him off. "You are just going to do what I tell you to do and answer my questions. Now for the last time, why were you on the marsh?"

Biter purposely dragged out the words as if this would help the lawman understand his meaning. "As I said before, I was MEASURRRINNG MYYYY CLAMMMS."

"OK, that's it," the officer yelled. "Turn around, get down on the ground and put your hands on your head."

As Biter complied, the sheriff's deputy came up swiftly behind him, pulled Biter's left arm forcefully behind his back and handcuffed his wrist. He then quickly grabbed his right arm, brought it behind his back and affixed the remaining shackle. He then proceeded to read Biter his Miranda rights.

When he was done, Biter said, "You've got to be kidding me. Is this some kind of a joke? What is it that you think I've done?"

"I'll ask the questions," the young officer said firmly. He got Biter back on his feet and led him back to his patrol car. When the two men got to the vehicle, the officer had Biter spread his legs and lean across the hood of the car. "Do you have any weapons, needles or other sharp objects in your possession that I need to know about?"

Biter shook his head in the negative, and the deputy initiated a pat down procedure to determine if he was telling the truth. As he did so, he detected the presence of a hard, metal object in the right pocket of Biter's jacket. "Sir, what's in your coat pocket?"

"Oh, that's just my calipers."

"What the hell are calipers?" The officer lost his patience and forced Biter's head forcefully down on the hood of the car. "Jesus! Why can't you just give me a straight answer for once?"

Biter was equally enraged. "That's police brutality! I've been telling you the truth. If you would just listen to me for a minute, you might understand what I'm saying."

The deputy reached into Biter's pocket and carefully removed the object in question. Seeing that it was not a knife as he had expected, the deputy regained his composure, placed the calipers on the car and continued his questioning. "Sir, do you have any controlled substances in your possession?"

"No," Biter said flatly.

The deputy reached inside Biter's hip waders and removed his wallet from the back pocket of his jeans. As he did so, Biter said, "You'll find my professor's business card in the left fold of my wallet with my other cards, or you can call his graduate student, Bailey Ford. I can give you his number as well. If you give them a call, they'll be able to verify my story."

The officer placed the wallet on the car's hood next to the calipers. "We'll check this out when we get back to the station."

The deputy removed the remaining contents from Biter's pockets and was relieved to find nothing of concern. He then led Biter to the right side of the car, opened the rear door, placed his hand on Biter's head and eased him into the back seat of the vehicle. The two then drove back to the station with Biter, continuing to demand an explanation for why he was being detained, and the deputy, refusing to provide Biter with specifics other than to tell him he was being transported to the station for further questioning.

TWENTY

While Biter was being fingerprinted at the station, the deputy walked over to the sheriff's office to tell him what had transpired since they last spoke on the radio and to confirm a plan of action. The sheriff, a gray-haired, overweight man in his late fifties, was working on a crossword puzzle from the local newspaper when the deputy entered his office.

"The suspect is being processed now," the young lawman said. "I called the kid's folks like you told me, and I'm going over there now to meet up with them. The boy and his Dad have agreed to accompany me to the spot where the kid found the body."

"Good," the sheriff replied. "I'm going in to question the suspect in a few minutes. Since he was leaving the marsh when you arrived on the scene, he has most likely already disposed of the body, but let me know what you find. Give me a call as soon as you have any new information."

"Will do, Sheriff."

Biter was led into a small room that was obviously outfitted for the sole purpose of interrogating suspects. The room was brightly lit, but there was nothing in it except for one rectangular, eight-foot table and four chairs. For the most part, the concrete walls of the room were devoid of any openings. The only exceptions were the door that led into the room and a large, reflective window that was located on the opposite wall. Biter guessed that the window was a one-way mirror. He had seen enough cop shows on TV to know that there was probably a darkly lit room on the other side of the glass where other officers were observing and videotaping him.

The attending officer removed the handcuffs from Biter's wrists and directed him to take a seat at the table. As he did so, the sheriff entered the room, and the junior officer walked over to meet him. The two policemen then engaged in a brief conversation out of Biter's range of hearing before returning to the table and taking their seats on the opposite side, directly in front of Biter. "Hello, Mr. Starypan," the sheriff said. "I'm Sheriff Mannion."

"Sheriff, is it? Well, good. Maybe I can get some answers from you. Your deputy refused to tell me what I'm being charged with."

The sheriff had a thin smile on his face, but his jaw muscles tightened noticeably when Biter began to speak, betraying his true feelings. "Calm down, Mr. Starypan. You have not yet been charged with a crime. As my deputy explained to you several times, at this stage in our investigation, you're just here for further questioning."

"But I didn't do anything wrong! What is it that you think I've done?"

"Sir, this will go a lot easier if you let me ask the questions and you just answer them to the best of your ability. What were you doing out there on the marsh?"

"I already answered this. As I told your deputy countless times, I was out there measuring my clams."

"You must understand that this sounds rather ludicrous. When my deputy arrived on the scene, you had a shovel and a pair of rubber gloves in a bucket. There were no clams."

"That's because I put them back. I already explained this to your dimwitted deputy! I'm a research assistant at the marine lab. I'm doing a growth study on clams. I asked your deputy several times to give my boss a call to verify what I'm saying is the truth. Did you even bother to call him?"

"We did. We called his office, and we just got his answering machine, which isn't surprising since today is Saturday. We also called his home, but there was no answer."

"So what are you going to do? Keep me here until Monday?"

"We'll keep you here as long as it takes to learn the truth," the sheriff countered. "You may indeed be a research assistant, but it doesn't explain the presence of a human corpse in the vicinity of where you were digging."

"Corpse? What are you taking about?"

"Let's cut to the chase. We have a witness who will testify that he saw you digging in the shallows and that there was the body of a dead human in close proximity to where you were digging. This places you directly in a crime scene. What is your relationship with the deceased?"

"I don't know what you're talking about. This is crazy! You think I'm a murderer? I know my rights. I'm not going to say anything further until I talk to a lawyer. I think you and your deputy are delusional and have seen way too many cop shows."

The junior officer piped up, "Let's try to keep this discussion respectful. If you're innocent, you have nothing to be concerned about."

"Oh, really? I'm being held against my will, and I'm supposed to be fine with that? No! There is no further discussion until I talk to a lawyer."

The sheriff struggled to conceal his anger, but his face became flushed with blood. "That's certainly within your rights. Do you have a lawyer you would like to contact or would you like us to provide you with a public defender?"

"I don't have a lawyer."

"Very well," the sheriff responded. "We are done here." He pushed back his chair, stood up and said to his junior officer, "See to it that this man has access to a public defender."

The sheriff had resumed work on his crossword puzzle when his deputy called him on the phone. He could tell from the young officer's voice that he was very upset. "What's wrong?"

"It looks like this guy is innocent after all," the deputy responded.

"You mean his cockamamie story is true?"

"It looks like it, sir," the deputy said nervously. "When we got to the site where the boy had originally found the body, it was still there. But the corpse was badly decomposed. It's obvious that it was in the ocean for some time before being washed up on the shore."

"Well that's just great," the sheriff said in disgust. "Why wasn't this information conveyed to us when the kid's parents first called us?"

"I asked his Dad the very same question. He said his son was really freaked out when he got home and that he and his wife had their hands full just trying to calm him down."

"So the parents never questioned the kid about the body?"

"That's affirmative," the deputy responded.

"If this guy goes to the local paper, we'll look like idiots. This is exactly the kind of story the local rag loves to disseminate."

"Sheriff, I know this looks like I overreacted, but when I arrived on the scene, the suspect was on his way off the marsh. I couldn't let him leave, and I was by myself, so I couldn't go out on the marsh and inspect the crime scene before taking him into custody."

The sheriff tried to comfort his deputy. "No, you did the right thing under the circumstances. But it makes us look like country yokels just the same. I hate that. I'll talk to you further when you get back to the station. Right now, I want to release the suspect as quickly as possible. It hasn't been a good day for this poor bastard either. I mean, the guy has done nothing wrong. He was just in the wrong place at the wrong time."

Biter heard the door to his holding cell being unlocked and sat up on the cot he had been lying on. The door opened, and the same policeman who had led him to the interrogation room was at the entrance. "Mr. Starypan, please come with me."

"Where are you taking me?"

"Back to processing to retrieve your personal property and then I'll transport you back to your vehicle."

"You mean I'm being released?"

"Yes."

Biter exploded. "That's it? After all you've put me through, don't you think you owe me an explanation?"

"I'm sorry, sir, but I'm not at liberty to discuss police matters."

"No, that's not good enough! You owe me some answers!"

"I'm sure you understand that we had to verify your story. After further investigation, we've determined you are telling the truth. We apologize for any inconvenience you may have suffered," the officer responded.

"May have suffered? You bring me here in handcuffs, tell me I'm a murder suspect and I'm supposed to be fine with that? I'm going to sue you for false arrest."

"With all due respect, sir, at no time were you under arrest. You were just here for further questioning. As I said before, we are truly sorry for your personal inconvenience, but we were just doing our job. If you'll just come with me, we'll retrieve your personal property and then I'll transport you back to your vehicle."

TWENTY—ONE

The front door to the Red Dragon swung open, and Biter entered. JT glanced at the clock above the bar. "Biter, you're early. Carl won't be in to relieve me for another hour yet."

"Yeah, I know. I wasn't doing anything, so I thought I'd come in to have a beer while I waited for you to get off work."

"Right on. You want your usual, I assume?"

"You know it," Biter said as he grabbed the stool next to Mac.

JT poured a glass of barleywine and slid it across the bar to his friend. Mac was reading the local newspaper and didn't bother to look up. "Hello, son, have you seen today's *Coastal Times*?"

"No. Why?"

"Because there's an article in it about your dead man," Mac replied.

Biter perked up and was obviously interested. Turning back a few pages, Mac found the story and started reading it aloud. "On Saturday, a ten-year-old boy, whose name has not been released at the request of his parents, found the body of a dead adult male while playing on Wyckham's Marsh. A spokesman for the sheriff's office has confirmed that the body was badly decomposed when the investigating officer arrived on the scene and that the department has determined that the death was not a homicide. Although authorities can't be certain until DNA and dental records are analyzed, they suspect that the body is that of a man who eyewitnesses had reported being swept into the ocean by a sneaker wave several months earlier. At the time of the incident, police had searched the surrounding waters but were unable to recover a body."

Biter was incensed. "That's why they let me go. Those hapless cops hadn't even inspected the body before they took me into custody. If they had, they would have seen that the body was months old. No killer would hold on to a corpse for that long."

Mac couldn't resist. "Ray, with all due respect, that's not necessarily the case. Don't you remember Jeffrey Dahmer and what the cops found in his refrigerator?"

Biter took the bait. "So you're telling me I look like a serial killer?"

"Well, you do have those shifty, little eyes," Mac said.

JT chuckled. "Mac's got a good point. You do have shifty, little eyes…and they do disappear when you laugh."

Biter's eyes widened, and his mouth dropped open. "I can't believe you are siding with Mac. Do I even know you?"

"Oh, lighten up," JT said. "I was just giving you shit. When did you stop being able to take a joke?" JT rubbed his forehead above his right eye. "Hey Biter, you mind doing me a favor? I've had this pain above my eye for a few hours, and I'm just now starting to get a splitting headache. I hate to take you away from your beer but would you mind taking over the bar until Carl gets here? I'd like to go in the back and lie down on the couch in Mai's office."

"No, of course I don't mind." As Biter stood up to go behind the bar, he saw that Mac's glass was empty and slid his beer over to him. "I've barely touched this. Do you want it?"

"Normally, I'm not a big fan of the barleywine," Mac replied. "But nothing tastes better than a free beer. I'll take it off your hands."

JT laughed as he rubbed the back of his neck. "You're a real prince, Mac."

Biter looked concerned. JT didn't look good. "Have you taken any painkillers?"

"No. The headache just started. I think Mai has a bottle of aspirin in her office."

"I hope you feel better, bro. Is there anything I can do to help?"

"You're doing it," JT answered. "You're watching the bar."

"I mean in addition to that."

"No, I'm OK. Just let me know when Carl gets here."

As JT headed toward the back of the bar, Mac asked Biter, "Does JT get migraines often?"

"No, not very often," Biter replied. "At least, not that I can remember."

"Well, he's lucky. I get them all the time."

Biter laughed. "Mac, yours aren't migraines. They're called hangovers."

Mac wasn't amused. "Son, I wasn't going to bring it up, but I have to admit that I was a little hurt that you didn't call me when the cops gave you the option to contact your lawyer."

"Oh really," Biter retorted. "Do you think that my lawyer calling me 'Ray' would have helped clear up the confusion with my situation?"

Mac laughed. "Come on, son. You're smarter than that. You know I would have dropped the 'Ray' thing if you had called me to represent you. I'm your friend, for fuck's sake. If you're ever in trouble in the future, please give me a call."

Biter realized he was serious. "Thanks, Mac. I should have called you. I guess I wasn't thinking straight."

Mac smiled. "It's always scary when you're dealing with the cops. But instead of dwelling on the negative aspects of your experience, I think you should embrace it. It's a great story! You know you love to tell stories to anyone who will listen. Lord knows, I and just about everyone else in this bar have heard all of yours ad nauseam. What is it that you always say when we try to stop you from telling us a story you've told countless times before?"

Biter smiled. "It's a quote from Groucho Marx: If you've heard this story before, don't stop me, because I'd like to hear it again."

Mac laughed heartily. "Exactly! Once the experience has aged awhile and the vulnerability you felt at the hands of the cops subsides, I know you'll love telling this story over and over again to anyone who'll listen." Mac let out a heavy sigh and yelled, "Oh, Jesus, Mary and Joseph, please help us all! I just realized we'll have to listen to this story over and over again. I just hope we'll at least get a free beer each time we have to endure it."

Biter raised his eyes. "Oh, and your stories are so riveting." He saw that Mac had already finished the barleywine. "Boy, you downed that pretty quick. The barleywine is nearly 12% alcohol. It's a lot stronger than that cheap beer you're used to."

"Don't worry about me. I can handle my alcohol just fine. I was drinking when you were still playing in the dirt."

Arnie and Will had just entered the bar and overheard Mac's last comment. As they took their seats, Will asked, "Yeah, you were probably, what? Fifteen years old at the time?"

Mac laughed. "I got a late start."

Biter just shook his head as he gave Arnie and Will their standard drinks. He heard the front door open and looked up.

As Carl walked up to the bar, he asked, "Biter, what are you doing behind the bar? I thought today was your day off?"

"It is. JT wasn't feeling well when I got here, so I've been manning the bar for him. He's in back on Mai's couch."

"What's wrong with him?"

"He's got a bad headache." Biter looked up at the clock. "You still have 10 minutes before your shift starts."

"Don't be stupid. Go get JT and get out of here. I've got it covered."

Biter smiled. "Thanks, Carl," he said, as he walked to the back of the bar. When he entered Mai's office, he saw JT lying on the couch. He shook him gently to wake him up. "Carl's here now. We can go home."

When there was no response, Biter became alarmed and shook him violently and screamed, "JT! Are you OK? Can you hear me?" Biter placed two fingers on his friend's carotid artery to feel for a pulse and lowered his ear above his friend's mouth to see if he was still breathing. When he could detect neither, he jumped up and ran to the front of the bar and screamed, "Call 911! JT is unconscious. He's not breathing!" Biter raced to the back of the bar, grabbed his friend off the couch, lowered him to the floor and began administering CPR.

Carl ran to the phone and called for help. He dispatched Arnie and Will to opposite ends of the street to flag the EMT personnel down when they arrived and directed Mac to watch the bar. He then hurried in back to help. "Biter, have you ever done CPR before?"

"No, but we had a class at the zoo," Biter shouted as he continued to work on JT.

"I was a medic in the army," Carl replied. "I've done this countless times before. Let me do it."

Biter wanted desperately to help his friend, but he understood Carl was JT's best chance for survival. He jumped up and let Carl take over. As Carl continued to press forcefully down on JT's chest, Biter stood nearby and watched helplessly. EMT personnel arrived in less than 10 minutes and took over performing CPR. As they continued to work on JT, another paramedic questioned Biter in an attempt to get vital information that might be helpful. "How old is your friend?"

"Thirty-five," Biter answered.

"Did you or anyone else see your friend collapse?"

"No. He said he had a bad headache and went in the back of the bar to lie down."

"How long would you estimate he was in the back?"

"Maybe forty minutes, max."

"Had he taken any drugs?"

"No, he was working. He's a bartender here."

"Do you know anything about his medical history?"

"I know he was hardly ever sick. He always seemed real healthy to me."

Biter watched as the paramedics continued to work on JT and loaded him into the vehicle for transport to the hospital. As they sped off, Biter ran to the front of the bar to get his car and follow the EMT truck to the hospital.

Carl stopped him. "Biter, you can't drive. You're too upset. Mac, can you give Biter a ride to the ER?"

"Of course," Mac answered. "Come with me son. You're in no condition to drive. I'll take you to the hospital."

TWENTY–TWO

Biter sat in the emergency room waiting area, nervously flipping through a magazine. By the speed with which he turned the pages, Mac could tell Biter wasn't even looking at the pictures. "Son, you need to get a hold of yourself. You're wound up like a top. You're making me nervous just watching you. The doctors are doing everything they can for JT. All we can do is pray and wait."

"We should have taken him to the hospital as soon as he didn't feel well."

"Don't go down that road, son. Woulda, coulda, shoulda—it's always a pointless and thankless exercise. No one could have known this would happen. People get headaches every day."

"But JT was never sick. I should have known something was wrong."

Mac became visibly angry. "Stop it, son! It's not your fault. What good is this self-flagellation? It doesn't help JT, and it's not healthy."

As Biter started to respond, he saw the nurse motioning to him to come up to the admittance desk. He and Mac walked up to the counter. "Mr. Starypan, the doctor would like to speak with you. Can you come with me?"

"Can my friend come too?"

The nurse at first hesitated but then saw the condition Biter was in and said, "I guess it's OK." She then led them to a small examination room behind the waiting area.

After they were seated, a physician entered the room. As they began to stand up, he introduced himself. "I'm Dr. Swartz. Please take a seat."

Biter continued standing and looked, nervously at the doctor. "Is my friend still alive?"

The doctor took a deep breath and let out a heavy sigh. "No. I'm sorry. He's gone. We did everything we could, but we couldn't revive him."

Biter collapsed back down in his chair, placed his head in his hands and started crying uncontrollably.

"Your friend had a cerebral aneurysm," the doctor said. "A brain aneurysm is—"

Biter cut him off and looked up. "I know what it is. The wall of a blood vessel in the brain balloons out for some reason and fills with blood."

"Precisely," the doctor said. "Your friend's aneurysm ruptured, and the blood entered his brain. An autopsy will determine whether the aneurysm was due to an earlier head injury or whether it was a congenital birth defect."

Biter stared at the doctor in disbelief with tears welling in his eyes. "What difference does it make? He'll still be dead!"

Mac rubbed Biter's back. "Come on, son, don't be disrespectful. The doctor is just doing his job."

"I know. I'm sorry," Biter replied.

"No apologies necessary," Dr. Swartz said. "I understand what you're going through. We've notified the deceased's parents, and they will determine the disposition of the body." As he started to leave the room, he stopped and turned back to face Biter. "I'm sorry. This is never easy. I assure you we did everything we could."

TWENTY-THREE

After a month, the fitful nights without quality sleep had left Biter lethargic and on edge, and the deep-seated pain he felt in the pit of his stomach was now ever present. His depression and heavy drinking had taken its toll. His face was gaunt. He had dark circles under his eyes, and he was noticeably underweight. He wanted to believe he would get better but felt there was no longer any hope of recovery. Not knowing what else to do, he decided to take matters into his own hands.

Biter grabbed a glass from the cupboard and a bottle of cabernet sauvignon from the wine rack and headed down the stairs to the garage. As he opened the door, he ran his hand along the right side of the wall, searching for the light switch. His fingers found their target, and his eyes took a moment to adjust to the light.

As he walked around the front of his Ford Ranger, he paused to assess the sad state of his rusty vehicle, and it struck him how different he really was from his departed friend. JT would go four-wheeling and come home with his Dodge Ram caked in mud. He would then spend hours washing and waxing his truck and polishing his rims.

Biter never understood the logic of this ritual. He couldn't remember the last time he washed his truck. It wasn't something that was important to him. The floor of his vehicle was littered with ATM receipts, loose change, remnants of potato chips and candy wrappers. JT and just about all of his other friends had loved to kid him about the slovenly state of his ride. He recalled his favorite comeback to this ribbing. "Hey," he'd say to anyone who hadn't heard his response before, "you could eat off the floor in my truck!"

Predictably, the person he was addressing would raise his eyes in disbelief. He'd then say, "I bet you could find enough food there to survive for a couple of weeks if you had to." It never failed to get a laugh, and it caused Biter to crack a weak smile even now as he thought about it.

Biter turned on the radio on the shelf above the workbench and located his favorite rock station. As Metallica's "Fade to Black" began to flow smoothly through the speakers, which were mounted on opposing walls of the garage, he removed a roll of duct tape from the upper drawer of the workbench and used it to seal off all of the openings around the garage door. He then got in the driver's seat of his truck and rolled down the windows on both sides of the cab. After starting the engine, he poured himself a glass of wine and then propped the bottle up next to him on the bench seat.

As Biter sat there sipping his wine, he couldn't help but notice the rubber fish staring back at him from its plaque on the wall above the keg cooler. Big Mouth Billy Bass had been there since JT's Dad had sent it to him as a gag years earlier. He smiled as he recalled how much of a kick he and JT had originally gotten out of this stupid, animatronic gadget the first time they heard it sing, "Take Me to the River, Put Me in the Water." He also recalled how quickly they had tired of it and had pulled the plug to stifle it.

He was struck by how much this mirrored his own experiences with the women he had dated. Early in a relationship, he'd be so smitten that he would initially only see the woman's good qualities. As time went on, however, he would become aware of her flaws, and the relationship would inevitably lose its luster. He knew that's why he was alone now. He was under no illusion that he was any prize himself, so he wondered why he held others up to a higher standard. Although he would never admit it, he knew the answer. The thought of making a lifetime commitment to any one individual scared the hell out of him, and he could never bring himself to do it. He knew that his inability to make a commitment was the reason for his and Cassandra's break-up.

At the same time, he believed some of his friends had gotten married only because they were afraid of the prospect of spending their lives alone. He didn't think the threat of loneliness was enough to justify a lifetime commitment to someone you were unsure was a good match. He was resolute that he had made the right choices, given the women he had encountered, but at the same time, he wondered what in his life he had missed because of it.

Carbon monoxide continued to spew from the truck's tailpipe as Biter pounded what wine was left in his glass and poured himself another. Taking a healthy swig, he stared through the windshield, searching the area of the garage within his field of view for something else to consume his thoughts. The room was filled with JT's stuff, and it seemed that just about every object his eyes made contact with reminded him of his departed friend. The tools strewn over the workbench, the crab rings stacked on the over-sized truck tires in the corner, the tackle boxes and fishing rods sitting next to them, and the kayak paddles propped against the far wall—all unleashed a string of vivid memories—Biter and JT crabbing on the bay; fishing for salmon and steelhead; and four-wheeling high up in the hills near dusk in an attempt to catch the last rays of the sun before it disappeared beyond the horizon. Each living memory cascaded into another as if they were competing for his attention.

He closed his eyes, and in his mind, Biter could see JT and himself paddling their kayaks upriver late one moonless, summer night. The flashlights they had placed in the front of their inflatable yellow boats transformed their vessels into river lanterns, providing the only light illuminating their paths. Bats, catching insects on the wing, skirted in and out of view as they darted back and forth through the muted cones of light their flashlights cast inches above the water's surface. The flickering, fleeting images of these winged mammals took on a zoetrope-like quality, and Biter recalled how surreal this seemed to him at the time. He knew words could not describe how much he cherished this memory and the countless others like it that he had shared with his best friend.

Biter realized he had taken their friendship for granted and only now fully appreciated how fortunate he had been to have known someone like JT. His friend had an adventuresome spirit and was a little crazy. Without someone like that to prod him out of his comfort zone, Biter knew he would have spent way too much time safely rooted to his favorite wingchair. JT had never been content to sit still. He had made up his mind that he would have fun every day, no matter what, and Biter had been lucky enough to be invited along for the ride.

Biter opened his eyes as "Oh Me" by Nirvana surfaced on the airwaves. His gaze now fixed on the dog bed that was mounted high on the wall. The bed had belonged to JT's miniature poodle, Bridget, which had died several years earlier. A framed picture of the silver-haired, little dog was mounted on the wall immediately beside it. Biter remembered the day Bridget had died and how much his friend had grieved over the loss of his pet. Even now, he could feel his friend's pain as he relived the moment. He recalled how much he had been touched by his friend's heartfelt demonstration of emotion. Growing up, Biter had been conditioned by his father to internalize his feelings, and he remembered how much he had envied JT's emotional freedom and lack of constraint.

Biter remembered how difficult it had been for his father to show any affection at all. He recalled a Christmas long past when his mother had encouraged him to give his father a kiss after he had opened his presents and how uncomfortable he sensed this had made his father feel. As a child, he thought his father's lack of affection was somehow his fault, and this had caused him considerable anguish. But as an adult, he now understood that his father was just a product of his upbringing, and he held no resentment for the man.

Biter's grandparents had come to America shortly after the Russian Revolution in 1917, and his father had grown up during the Great Depression and had no warm memories of his childhood. From as early as his father could remember, life was something you just had to get through. His father left home at sixteen as much to escape his parents as he did to exert his independence. He joined FDR's Civilian Conservation Corps, and Biter remembered how frequently and fondly his father had reminisced about his time in the CCC. As a young man, hearing his father's stories of glory days gone by, Biter sensed sadly that this was the high point of his father's life.

He now understood that his father had seen life as something you had to endure rather than something you should embrace. He felt pity for this perspective, but he understood instinctively that his father's perceived coldness was actually a sign of love. His father saw emotion as a weakness and wanted his son to be strong and survive. In this context, his father's actions were totally understandable, but as a child, this awareness had escaped him. He wished he had the luxury of telling his father now that he understood his motivation for his lack of affection that Christmas so many years ago. He grudgingly accepted the sad reality that this was no longer possible and that his negative experiences had molded him as a man and made him his father's son.

Biter knew that before JT's death no one had seen him cry in ten years or more. Now it seemed like he couldn't stop crying. Even the smallest thing he found beautiful or incredibly sad in some way seemed to open up the floodgates. It had happened to him in the grocery store just yesterday. He was at the checkout counter when James Taylor's version of Carol King's song, "You've Got a Friend," started playing over the store's loudspeakers. He always loved this song, but, for some reason, it now took on a larger importance. He tried to control himself but was powerless to stop the tears that streamed down his face. Just as he was about to bolt from the store in embarrassment, he heard JT's voice in his head. "Well, well," JT said, laughing with approval. "You've come a long way, Biter. You've learned compassion. I'm proud of you."

Hearing his friend's words and laughter brought a smile to his face, and he started laughing as well. Biter knew he must have looked like a raving lunatic, laughing and crying at the same time. Seeing the frightened look on the checker's face confirmed this and made him laugh even louder. He wanted to tell her that the tears he now shed were derived from joy, not sadness, but for some reason, he no longer felt self-conscious or compelled to explain himself. Instead, he paid his bill and left the store thankful for the brief telepathic communication he had with his friend and with an even greater longing to see him again.

Biter knew that he and JT were alike and, at the same time, different in so many ways. Sometimes it felt like they could read each other's thoughts. Other times, it felt like they were diametrically opposed and would end their relationship with one of them killing the other. However, the amazing thing was that no matter how much either one of them had done to destroy their friendship, it seemed like there was nothing either one of them could do to end it.

Biter realized that, at the time, both he and JT thought whatever issue they were arguing about seemed important, but the fact that he couldn't remember the source of even one argument now was evidence that their scrapes were inconsequential. It was as if their fights had, in some inexplicable way, melded their friendship and made it stronger. This had not been his experience with any of the other friends with which he had had a falling out. He recalled those friends he had abandoned with sadness, and he acknowledged that there were probably an equal number who had jettisoned him for some slight they felt he had committed.

What is the chemistry, Biter wondered, that brings two people together, who are seemingly so different, to become such close friends? He had known JT for about seventeen years, but he felt like he and JT went back a lot further. Viscerally, he felt that they had shared countless experiences his mind could not recall. Could it be that they had shared past lives together? If that were the case, he couldn't wait for their next adventure to begin. His decision to end his life never seemed more right than it did at this moment. He longed to see his deceased friend again, and perhaps, most of all, he was anxious to learn whether his belief in an afterlife was real.

Carbon monoxide continued to consume the garage, and the colorless, odorless gas was beginning to make Biter light-headed and sleepy. Suddenly his truck started shaking violently, the lights in the garage began flickering on and off, and the music on the radio was consumed by static. Biter pumped the gas pedal to see if this would stop his truck's convulsions, but the engine continued to shake for several seconds before finally sputtering to a halt. At the same time, the lights in the garage went out, and the radio went mute.

Biter attempted to restart the vehicle several times with no success. After turning the ignition key off, he set his wine glass down carefully in the cup holder on the dash and reached into the glove box to retrieve the flashlight he kept there for emergencies. Armed with this light source, he exited the vehicle. He could see no logical connection between the power failure and his vehicle's malfunction. What a weird coincidence, he thought to himself.

As he made his way across the front of his truck, a shaft of silver light shot suddenly through the window on his left, illuminating his path. Biter turned to the window and saw JT's image in the glass in front of him!

Startled, Biter jumped backwards, lost his footing, and dropped the flashlight. As he fell to the floor, he could hear his friend laughing heartily. He recognized JT's characteristic laugh and knew instantly that this was, indeed, his old friend!

Struggling to his feet, Biter gasped in amazement, "I'm not crazy! It really is you!" Shaking, not in fear but excitement, he stared at his friend's image in the window.

"I'm sorry, Biter," JT said. "I didn't mean to laugh at you, but you looked like a turtle, struggling to get off its back." JT's smile faded, and his face suddenly grew somber. "Biter, you're a mess. What are you thinking? You can't take your own life. You know it's wrong."

"I don't want to live anymore," Biter countered as tears began streaming profusely down his face. "Don't you know how much I miss you?"

Biter saw the pain on JT's face, and he immediately regretted his outburst.

"Oh Biter, my dear friend," JT said sadly. "Of course, I do. You know I do. Why do you think I'm here? It hurts me that my death has caused you such anguish, and I can't bear to see you beating yourself up like this. It wasn't my choice to die, but it was my time. This isn't yours. I'm at peace, and I want you to find peace as well. You can't cut your time short. You still have something important to do in this life."

"What do you mean? I don't understand," Biter said weakly.

JT's image began to fade, and Biter knew instinctively that the communication was ending. He placed his hands gently on the windowpane, closed his eyes, and sobbed softly, "Don't go. Please don't go!"

When Biter opened his eyes, JT was gone. Where his friend's image had been, a full moon now filled the windowpane. Seeing the celestial body, Biter's first inclination was to question whether JT's visitation had, in fact, actually occurred. His mind told him that, given his troubled mental state, the experience could easily just have been a figment of his imagination. In his heart, however, there was no such doubt, and he knew instinctively that the encounter was real.

Biter picked up his flashlight from the floor and walked slowly to the electrical panel. As he opened the door of the gray metal box, he saw that the main power breaker had tripped. He flipped the switch, and the lights instantly came back on, and the radio once again found its voice. He knew that this still did not explain his truck's simultaneous malfunction.

Standing there silently, he struggled to find a scientific explanation for what he had experienced. It was clear to him that JT had orchestrated both the power outage and his car's failure in an attempt to prevent him from taking his own life, but how was this possible? As he contemplated this, he suddenly became aware of the music playing on the radio and recognized the song immediately. It was Alice in Chains' "Rotten Apple":

"What I see is unreal
I've written my own part
Eat of the apple, so young
I'm crawling back to start"

Biter got back in his truck and turned the ignition key clockwise to see if the vehicle would start. The engine sprung easily to life and started purring smoothly as if nothing had been wrong. "How very strange," he whispered to himself as he continued to listen to the music.

Biter reached for his wine glass in the cup holder but then thought better of it and withdrew his hand. As the song ended, he sat in his truck motionless for several minutes, reliving his brief encounter with his friend. Tears once again started slowly running down his face and then turned into a torrent. Biter was emotionally conflicted. The elation he derived from seeing his departed friend was offset by the cold reality of how empty his life now seemed without him. He shut the engine off and exited his vehicle.

As he made his way around the front of his truck, he turned off the radio and walked over to the door leading up to the main house. Opening the door, he shut off the lights and walked up the stairs to his bedroom. As he lay on his bed, Layne Staley's voice continued to haunt him. The words, "I'm crawling back to start," played over and over in his mind as he stared up at the ceiling. He closed his eyes and tried to fall asleep, but his mind leaped haphazardly from one thought to another. What did JT mean when he said I still have something important to do in this life? Is it one last selfless act I have to perform, or do I still have an important lesson to learn? As he lay there contemplating these questions, exhaustion overtook him, and he drifted off to sleep.

TWENTY–FOUR

The incessant ringing of the downstairs telephone brought Biter back to life, but the splitting headache he awakened to was nearly unbearable, and it made him wish that he were dead. He knew he hadn't drunk enough wine to cause a headache of this caliber and that the excruciating pain above his eyes was due, not to his alcohol consumption, but to his near carbon monoxide poisoning the night before.

What dumb ass would call me this early in the morning, he thought angrily to himself. Opening his eyes, he raised his torso off the bed and suddenly realized that his bedroom was awash in sunlight. He glanced at the clock on the nightstand and saw that it was nearly noon. As he got out of bed and slowly made his way down the stairs, he felt a little dizzy and grabbed onto the handrail for support. "I'm coming, I'm coming," he yelled pointlessly to no one. He had to endure several more rings before he finally made it to the phone. Picking up the receiver, he barked, "Hello." There was silence for a brief moment, and Biter realized that his greeting had, perhaps, been a bit too belligerent.

"Hello son. This is Mac, from the bar. Am I catching you at a bad time?"

Biter recognized the thick Scottish accent immediately. "I'm sorry if I screamed into the receiver, Mac. I was asleep when the phone rang, and I was just hurrying to pick it up."

"No worries, son. This is not a social call. Allow me to explain the reason for my disturbance. I don't know if you are aware of it or not, but JT had me draw up a will for him a while back. He named you as one of his beneficiaries."

Biter was dumbfounded. "No, this is the first I've heard of it. He never said anything to me about a will."

"Well, as the executor of his estate, it's my job to see that his property and other assets are distributed according to his wishes. Normally, I'd take care of this kind of thing over the phone, but in your case, I'd prefer to discuss this face to face. Would you be able to come to my office this afternoon?"

Biter was still at a loss for words. "Yeah, I guess. What time would you want me there?"

"I have an opening at 2 p.m. Would that work for you?"

Biter glanced up at the clock above the kitchen sink. "Yeah, that gives me enough time to take a shower and get over there. I'll see you then."

He hung up the phone and walked to the bathroom. After emptying his bladder, he opened the medicine cabinet, grabbed a bottle of aspirin and emptied six tablets into the palm of his hand. Downing these with a little water, he looked up and stared at his image in the mirror. JT was right, he thought. I am a mess.

TWENTY—FIVE

When Biter arrived at Mac's office, the sign on the door gave him pause. Silk screened on the glass were the words: The Mackenzie Law Firm, P.C. He realized that he only knew Mac from his interaction with his friends in the pub and that he really had never observed him in a professional setting. He wondered what effect, if any, meeting him now in his element would have on their personal dynamics. He looked down at his watch and realized he was already ten minutes late. He opened the door and walked up to the receptionist. "I'm afraid I'm a little tardy. I had a two o'clock appointment with Mr. Mackenzie."

"Yes. We've been expecting you, Mr. Starypan. Please take a seat. I'll let Mr. Mackenzie know you're here."

Biter was still searching for a magazine when the receptionist called him back to her desk. "Mr. Mackenzie will see you now. Please come with me."

Biter followed her dutifully down a long, narrow hallway. There was a single office door on each side and one at the end of the corridor. Before they had made it to the end of the hall, the last office door opened, and Mac stepped out with his arms extended. Giving Biter a big hug, he said, "Hello, son. Thanks for coming. Please come in." Closing the door behind them, Mac motioned for Biter to take a seat.

On the wall behind the large mahogany desk were the obligatory diplomas and professional awards that Biter knew were meant to convey Mac's bonafides within the legal system. The large window on his right offered an impressive floor-to-ceiling view of the Newport Bridge in the distance. Although he would never have admitted it, Biter had to grudgingly concede that, in this setting, Mac cut an imposing figure.

Mac plopped his large frame down on the leather chair on the other side of the desk. Sighing heavily, he looked up at Biter and said, "Son, I'm so sorry for your loss. I know how close you and JT were, and I know how I'd feel if I lost my best friend, Rex."

Biter struggled to maintain his composure. "Thanks, Mac. I really appreciate your concern. It means a lot to me."

"We've missed you at the bar. Mai told me you wanted to quit, but that she convinced you to take a few weeks off. I hope you're planning on coming back."

Biter looked down. "To be honest, Mac, I'm just taking it one day at a time right now."

"That's wise. I know you don't think so now, but time really is the great healer." Mac opened the lower drawer on the right side of his desk and withdrew a bottle of twelve-year-old scotch and a couple of empty shot glasses. Filling both, he handed one to Biter, raised his glass and said, "Here's to JT."

Biter grabbed the glass, and the two men toasted to their departed friend.

"Trust me," Mac said. "You'll never stop missing JT, and the pain of your loss will never completely go away, but, over time, it will subside."

Biter bit his lower lip. "That's a nice thought. I wish I could believe that."

Not knowing what else to say, Mac turned to the business at hand. "Well, maybe the news I have for you will be the beginning of your healing process. As I said on the phone, JT had me draw up a will for him, and he named you as one of the people who have claim to his estate. One of my duties as executor is to keep you informed of the progress of the probate process. I sent you a letter several weeks ago, but I received no response."

Biter looked directly at Mac and laughed weakly. "Yeah, well, that's not too surprising. Since JT died, the mail has been stacking up."

"Well, the good news is that there were no back taxes or creditor issues that needed to be resolved, and I'm now free to pass on to JT's heirs what he wanted them to have. I asked you to come here because JT left you his house on the river. It's yours."

Biter was numb and didn't respond.

Mac continued, "He also named you as the beneficiary of a $250,000 life insurance policy."

Biter was torn between elation and guilt. He was elated that he would now be able to stay in the house he had come to love, but he felt guilty that his newfound good fortune was made possible only by the death of his best friend. He looked down at his lap.

Mac waited for a response. When none was forthcoming, he asked gently, "Son, did you hear what I said?"

Biter looked up at Mac with a sad smile. "I heard you fine. I'm just trying to take it all in. That's all."

"I know it's a lot to absorb, but I thought you'd be pleased by the news."

"Don't get me wrong. It's an incredible gift, but I hate the thought of profiting from my best friend's death. It makes me feel dirty, like it's blood money or something."

Mac saw the pain and confusion on Biter's face and chose his words carefully. "With all due respect, I think your grief is clouding your better judgment. JT knew how much you love that house on the river, and he wanted you to have it in the event of his death. He also saw the insurance policy as a way to leave you a little nest egg. It's a testament to how much he cared about you and valued your friendship. I think that's something to celebrate, don't you?"

"When you portray it that way, I guess you're right. I'll keep the house, but I still don't feel right about taking the insurance money. I think I want to donate it to charity in JT's name."

"I don't think you should make any rash decisions," Mac said gently. "I think the best way to honor JT is to use your bequest as he intended. He wanted the proceeds from the insurance policy to provide for your long-term security. I'm sure donating the money to charity would give you some instant gratification, but it certainly wouldn't be what JT intended. If you give it away, it seems to me you're going against his wishes."

"Then what would you suggest I do with it? Put it in the bank or invest it in the stock market?"

"I think you should let some time pass before making any decision on what to do with the money. I'm not an investment lawyer, so if I were you, I wouldn't look to me for advice on what would be a good investment. I do, however, have some information that might interest you. You know that Mai is one of my clients as well. She, like all of us, was devastated by JT's death. I know for a fact that she's ready to retire and that she'd like to sell the bar to you if you are interested. I don't think it would be ethical for me to advise you pro or con on this business decision, but I know how much you and JT both loved the bar, and I see a certain symmetry in you being its next owner. It's just a thought, and like I said earlier, I wouldn't be too hasty in making any decisions for a while yet. It's just something to consider."

TWENTY—SIX

Returning home from his meeting with Mac, Biter went to the kitchen and took a frosty bottle of Jägermeister out of the freezer. As he walked to the cupboard to retrieve a glass, he glanced at the mound of dirty dishes in the sink in front of him, and this brought back memories of his brief stint as a dishwasher. In his mind, he relived his encounter with Mickey and recalled what JT had said to him about this at the time—that all the people we meet in our lives affect our spiritual development in some way. He remembered his experiences with the widower Buzz and Mac's friend Rex, and, for the first time, he grasped how much he had learned from these people in the past two years. He was humbled by the realization that it was those he had discounted, those that he had pitied in some way, or those that he had felt superior to, who, in retrospect, had taught him so much and had made him a more compassionate person.

And now this realization made him feel so small. As he started to cry, Biter, in his mind's eye, could see JT smiling approvingly at his newfound understanding. An incredibly calm feeling overtook him, and, for the first time since JT's death, he felt at peace with himself.

Biter opened the cupboard and saw that it was nearly empty. The only drinking vessel was a yellow, plastic camping cup on the upper shelf of the cabinet. He filled the cup with the dark brown liqueur and went out onto the deck and settled into a chair. As he sat there, staring out on the river and sipping his drink, he tried to make some sense of all that had happened to him in the last twenty-four hours.

JT had told him that he still had something important to do in his life. Should he give the insurance money to charity in JT's name? It would certainly be a fitting way for him to honor his friend, and it might just be the one truly selfless act he would perform in his life. Or was Mac right—that the best way to honor his friend was using the money the way JT had intended? Maybe buying the bar was really what JT would have wanted him to do?

As he sat there contemplating these questions, a tiger swallowtail butterfly flew over his head and landed on the lip of his cup, seemingly out of nowhere. Biter froze instantly so as not to frighten the insect away. He watched intently as the beautiful yellow-and-black striped butterfly unfurled its proboscis and began to drink the licorice-flavored nectar from his cup.

After a few minutes the butterfly had had its fill and abruptly took flight. Biter watched the swallowtail's trajectory as it flew erratically out over the river and then, unexpectedly, plummeted straight down into the water on the far side of the river!

Without thinking, Biter immediately ran down to the dock and dove into the river to save the butterfly. He wasn't a good swimmer, and the water was much colder and the current was far stronger than he had anticipated. He kept his eyes fixed on the swallowtail as he swam manically to where the insect was stranded. When he got to the butterfly, he began to tread water and slowly raised his right forearm underneath the swallowtail and gently lifted it from the river. Placing the two middle fingers of his left hand gently under the legs of the insect, he transferred it to the top of his head and started to swim toward the shore.

Suddenly he felt a sharp pain in his chest! He had never experienced such excruciating pain in his life before, and he had difficulty breathing. He gasped for air frantically as he clutched his chest. The piercing pain beneath his breastbone continued as he thrashed around wildly in the water in an effort to keep his head above the surface. All the while, the butterfly clung stubbornly to his hair, seemingly unconcerned.

As Biter's chest continued to explode in spasms of intense pain, he struggled feverishly to make it to the far shore. Less than twenty-four hours ago, he wanted to kill himself, and now he was summoning up every last ounce of energy he had in his body to survive. He knew there was no way that he could make it to the bank. "Please, God," Biter implored. "If there was ever a time in my life when I needed your help, it's now!"

His energy expended, Biter stopped swimming, and his body slowly started to sink in the water. As he lost consciousness, the tiger swallowtail took flight and flew skyward with newfound strength. It landed on the outer reaches of a branch of a bigleaf maple overlooking the river. As the insect sat there, slowly opening and closing its delicate, scaled wings, the sound of the rushing river reverberated off the surrounding hills like the sustained applause of an approving audience.

TWENTY—SEVEN

Biter opened his eyes and saw an old man with a weathered face and long, white hair, staring down at him. The stranger was tall, but slight of build, and he was dressed in a white robe. Biter was disoriented and asked sheepishly, "Are you Saint Peter?"

The old man's blue eyes grew big, and he started to laugh, "Oh, my stars, no! I'm your neighbor or, more accurately, I'm JT's neighbor. You don't know me, but I've seen you before. I know you've been living at JT's place for a while now. Are you alright?"

"I don't know if I'm alright. I'm not sure what happened to me. I think I may have had a heart attack."

"Then we better get you to the hospital. Are you in pain now?"

"No, I mean my chest is real sore, but the pain isn't as excruciating as it was."

"Well, that's encouraging," the old man said. He helped Biter up, and as they slowly made their way to the boat, he explained the reason for his attire. "I was out working in the yard all day and had just gotten into the shower when my six-year-old granddaughter came into the house screaming that you were lying on the ground on the other side of the river. I immediately called for an ambulance and came over in my boat as fast as I could. I knew every second was potentially critical so I didn't take the time to dress."

Biter started coughing violently, bent over and grabbed his chest. The old man became alarmed. "Are you alright? Are you having another attack?"

Biter straightened up. "I don't know. I just felt a sharp pain below my breastbone, but it's gone now."

"Hang on," the old man said. "Just a few more steps and we'll be to the boat."

When they got to the vessel, the old man helped Biter in and waited for him to take a seat before pushing the boat off the bank and hopping in. As they raced across the river, Biter just sat in the chair next to the old man, clutching his chest.

"We're almost to my house," the old man assured him. "It won't be long before the ambulance gets here."

When they got to his dock, the old man secured the boat and struggled to help Biter up the steep bank. As they slowly made their way up the hill, they could hear the emergency vehicle's siren growing ever louder. Just as they made it to the front of the house, the ambulance, with its lights flashing, came around the bend in the road and screeched to a halt in the driveway.

TWENTY-EIGHT

With a pillow propped up behind him, Biter sat in an upright position in his bed in the hospital's ER and stared blankly at the television that was mounted on the wall near the entrance to his room. Nothing caught his interest as he used the remote to surf through the channels, and he was getting impatient. The drugs the nurse had given him had alleviated his chest pain, but he was still incredibly weak. How long was he going to have to sit here, he thought, waiting for the prognosis from the doctor? He wanted to go home. He had been subjected to a barrage of diagnostic tests to determine what was wrong with him. Why was it taking so long, he wondered, for the doctor to share with him the results of all the tests he had undergone?

Just then the pastel blue curtain swung open and the cardiologist who had examined him earlier entered the room. "Hello, Mr. Starypan. How are you feeling right now? Are you experiencing any pain?"

"No, the meds the nurse gave me seem to be working fine, but I'm extremely tired."

"That's to be expected," the doctor said. "Well, I've got some good news for you. Your heart enzymes all look good, and your electrocardiogram showed no signs of a heart attack. We believe the source of your chest pain is acute pericarditis."

Biter looked quizzically at the doctor who continued his explanation. "There is a two-layered, fluid-filled sac, surrounding the heart, called the pericardium. Sometimes this sac becomes inflamed, and the resulting chest pain mimics a heart attack."

"What's the cause?"

"There are a whole host of possible causes. In young, healthy people like you, a viral infection is often the culprit. Have you had any gastrointestinal problems or flu-like symptoms in the past few weeks?"

Biter knew he could easily have had some kind of a bug and that he would never have known it. He had been drinking so heavily since JT died that he assumed the nausea and diarrhea he had experienced recently were just due to his excessive alcohol intake. He knew he should tell the doctor the truth, but he wasn't in the mood for a lecture so he lied, "No, not that I can remember."

"Well, in your case, it may be idiopathic."

"Is that bad?"

The doctor chuckled. "No, it's just a clinical way of saying we don't know the cause."

Biter was confused. "How can you treat the problem, if you don't know what caused it?"

"The blood samples we took will tell us whether the source of your pericarditis is bacterial. If it is, I'll prescribe a regimen of antibiotics. If it's not, you should need nothing more than some rest and treatment with aspirin or ibuprofen to reduce the inflammation and alleviate the pain. If that doesn't work, I'll prescribe something stronger. Most people with pericarditis fully recover in a few weeks. I have no reason to believe you will be any different, so I see no reason to keep you here any longer. You can go home. The nurse will be in shortly to help you get ready to leave the hospital." The doctor shook Biter's hand and exited the room.

Biter was overjoyed that he would soon be going home, but he was extremely exhausted and longed to get some sleep. He turned off the TV and closed his eyes. As he started to nod off, he felt the foot of his bed depress as if someone had just sat down on it. He opened his eyes and saw JT!

Smiling broadly and shaking his head slowly from side to side, JT said, "Biter, you suffer with such panache! I told you, you can't die yet. It's not your time. You've come a long way, I'll give you that, but you still have something important to do and to learn."

Biter started to speak, but JT cut him off. "You'll have to find out what that is for yourself. Oh, and by the way, saving the butterfly, while a noble act, was not selfless. You got the poor insect drunk after all." JT began to laugh heartily. Biter couldn't help himself and started laughing as well.

Just then a nurse entered the room, and Biter turned to face her. When the woman registered no surprise, he realized she didn't see his friend, and he quickly turned back to face JT, but he was gone.

The nurse had heard Biter laughing. "Did the doctor tell you that you can go home? Is that why you're so happy?"

"No. I mean, yes," Biter stammered. "The doctor said I could go home, but that's not why I'm in a good mood. I was just thinking of a dear, old friend. He always had the ability to make me laugh."

"Well, you can get dressed now," the nurse said.

"I'm afraid you are going to have to call me a cab. I don't have anyone to pick me up."

"Don't be silly," the nurse chided him. "Your neighbor is in the waiting room. He's been sitting there for hours."

Biter assumed it must be the old man who had come to his aid. "Is he an old guy in a white robe?"

The nurse started to giggle. "He's an older gentleman, but I don't remember him wearing a robe."

"Yeah, that makes sense," Biter said. "I've been here for a while now. I'm sure he had more than enough time to change his clothes."

The nurse continued to laugh as she lowered the railing on the side of the bed. "Your clothes are on the chair next to the door. Get dressed, and I'll be back in a few minutes to take you to meet your friend."

As Biter was being transported in a wheelchair down the long hallway leading to the hospital's entrance, he could see that the sun was setting and that JT's neighbor was patiently waiting for him outside in front of a red pickup. The lanky, old man was dressed in a T-shirt and jeans. Biter smiled to himself as he remembered their earlier meeting. When the front door opened and the two men were reunited, Biter said, "Based on the way you are dressed, it must be Casual Friday up at the Pearly Gates."

The old man looked confused. "I'm sorry. I don't understand."

"The last time I saw you, you were dressed in a robe, and I thought you were Saint Peter."

The old man laughed. "Oh, that's right! I was wearing my bathrobe." Extending his hand, he said, "In all the excitement, I never got your name. I'm Bob."

Biter grasped his hand. "My friends call me Biter."

The old man chuckled. "Oh, so you're Biter! JT told me a few stories about you."

Biter smiled broadly. "All lies, I'm sure. I deny everything."

Bob laughed heartily as he opened the passenger door and waited for Biter to get in. When the old man was back in the driver's seat, Biter turned to face him and said, "Seriously, I want to thank you for your kindness. You coming to the hospital to check on my condition and waiting all those hours is incredibly generous. I can't thank you enough."

As Bob started the vehicle and headed for home, he replied, "I didn't do anything you wouldn't have done if you were in my position."

"Then I guess JT really didn't tell you that much about me," Biter joked, only half-heartedly.

"I think you are being too hard on yourself," Bob countered. "I knew JT, and he was a good judge of character. If he didn't see some redeeming qualities in you, I don't believe he would have sent me to help you."

Biter's eyes widened noticeably. "What do you mean?"

Bob's face grew serious. "When I encountered you, time was of the essence, so I didn't elaborate. I told you my six-year-old granddaughter came into the house screaming that she saw you lying on the ground on the other side of the river. What I didn't share with you at the time was that she also said she saw Uncle JT standing over you and motioning to her like he needed help. I went out on the deck to see what she was talking about, but all I saw was you, lying there on the ground, on the far side of the river."

"That's quite incredible! You do know that JT passed away over a month ago?"

"Yes, I know," Bob said with remorse. "JT was always kind to my granddaughter, and she loved him dearly. I guess I didn't have the heart to tell her he was gone."

"No. That's not what I mean," Biter protested. "How do you explain what she saw?"

Bob smiled knowingly. "I'm an old man. Over the years, I've encountered a lot of things I couldn't explain. I've gradually come to accept the realization that life is a lot easier if you just take things at face value. You can call me crazy, but I truly believe my granddaughter saw your friend and that he wanted me to help you."

Biter said nothing, but he was secretly excited by this news. The fact that the little girl had also seen JT meant he wasn't going crazy! He knew in his heart that JT was still watching out for him—even in death!

After several minutes without a response, Bob looked over at Biter and saw him staring out the passenger window. "I'm sorry if I upset you."

Biter turned to Bob. "No! What you told me gives me great comfort, but, as you can imagine, it also makes me miss my friend just that much more."

"Understood," Bob said sadly. "If you don't mind me asking, what are you going to do now?"

"Funny you should ask. Twenty-four hours ago, I didn't have a clue, but after today's events, I think I'm getting close to making a decision on what I need to do with my life. For starters, it looks like you and I are going to be neighbors."

TWENTY-NINE

A couple of weeks later, when he was feeling better, Biter called Mai at the bar to let her know he was ready to come back to work if she still had an opening for him.

"Yes, of course," she assured him. "Carl and the other bartenders have been covering your shift while you were gone, and I'm sure they'll be overjoyed to finally get back to a normal schedule. Carl has worked over two weeks in a row now, and I know he's desperately in need of a break. Can you come in tomorrow to cover his shift?"

"I'm happy to work whatever hours you need me. If the truth be known, I actually think it will be good therapy for me."

"We've all been worried about you. I'm so pleased you're coming back, and I know the regulars will be happy to see you as well."

Biter became choked up and pretended to cough to hide his emotions.

Mai wasn't fooled for a minute. "Are you sure, you're OK?"

"Yes, I really think I am."

"Good. I'll see you tomorrow then."

Before she could hang up, Biter said, "Mac told me you were thinking about selling the bar. Were you serious?"

"Yes. I'm ready to retire. Are you interested?"

"Mac wasn't specific on the price, but if I can afford it, I think I am."

"Nothing would please me more than to sell it to you. I had hoped to sell it to JT one day."

Biter again struggled to control his emotions. After an awkward moment of silence, he said, "Well, good. I'll call Mac, and we'll see where it goes from there. Thanks again for being so understanding and saving a place for me."

"No thanks are needed. We are all family here. I'll see you tomorrow."

Biter's first day back to work was like a homecoming, and the bar that night was packed with customers. He guessed that Mai or Carl had called all the regulars to ensure a good showing. Even so, he was amazed by the turnout and touched by the enthusiasm with which his return was greeted by the locals.

The next day Biter contacted Mac to inform him of his interest in the business, and, to his surprise, the asking price was less than he had anticipated. He knew the amount of money the bar raked in on a daily basis, and he believed the price was more than fair. The sale went off without a hitch, and six weeks later, Biter was the new owner of the Red Dragon. He had no doubt that his decision to buy the bar was the right one. Nothing in his life had ever gone so smoothly, and he took the ease with which this transaction was completed as a sign that this was, in fact, what JT wanted him to do.

Some of the regulars encouraged Biter to change the name of the bar to "Tirebiter's." Not surprisingly, Mac disagreed and suggested he call it "Ray's Place." Biter was reluctant to change the name for two reasons. The one he often cited and which made the most sense financially was that the bar already had a good following, and he didn't want to do anything to hurt the business. The second reason was one Biter rarely mentioned, but was, in fact, the reason that carried the most weight. The bar had been called the Red Dragon when he and JT first started going there as customers. It was called the Red Dragon when JT starting working there, and it was still called the Red Dragon when he became a bartender as well. He and JT had shared countless good times in the Red Dragon, and he wanted to honor those memories by preserving the name.

Since he enjoyed interacting with the regulars, Biter continued to tend bar and kept the same work schedule he had as an employee. To his delight, Mai continued to frequent the bar for a few hours nearly every day as well, and as "Bar Owner Emeritus," she continued to receive her complimentary, "bottomless" rocks glass of bourbon, cracked ice and bitters. While in the bar, she also continued to control the remote and the movies that were shown on the bar's big screen TV. Biter had always been resistant to change, and he was pleased that things had really not changed that much since he had taken over ownership of the bar.

The only impending change of any significance was that Mai's long-time cook, Gus, who was in his late sixties, was about to retire. Biter knew his exit could potentially be a loss for the bar if he didn't pick the right person to replace him. Over the years, the locals had gotten used to Gus's cooking. Admittedly, the food Gus prepared wasn't fine cuisine, but it was good-tasting, consistent in quality and served in generous portions. Biter understood that whoever he chose to fill Gus's position would have to match this standard if the bar was to be successful in retaining its loyal clientele.

As he mulled over potential candidates—former employees and bar regulars he knew who were looking for employment—one man who fit neither of these categories kept coming to mind. Biter initially tried to dismiss him as an improbable choice, but, for some strange reason, the image of this man kept resurfacing in his mind, and he sensed that this was a sign he could not ignore. He felt compelled to act. He grabbed his jacket from the coat rack and said, "Carl, I'm going out for about an hour or so.

I think I may have found a good candidate to be our new cook, and I want to see if he's interested in the position."

"It would be a lot faster if you just called him on the phone," Carl said sarcastically.

"Yeah, if I had his number," Biter said as he exited the bar.

THIRTY

Biter waited patiently in the buffet line as he slowly worked his way up to the cashier. When he got to the front of the line, he paid for his meal and entered the dining room. To his relief, the person carving the prime rib and roast turkey was someone he did not recognize. He knew that he had been gone for a while and the likelihood of him running into someone he knew here was slim. Even so, he didn't want to take any chances and chose a table as far away from the serving line as possible.

Biter focused his attention on the door behind the buffet line and waited anxiously to see who would emerge from the kitchen. He wasn't even sure whether the person he had come to see still worked here, but this was the only place he knew where he could find him.

After a fifteen-minute wait, Biter felt he was wasting his time and stood up to leave. Just then, the door to the kitchen swung open, and Mickey entered the dining room with a load of dishes. Biter walked briskly to the beginning of the buffet line where his former co-worker was unloading his burden. "Excuse me, but does Queen still work here or have you made good on your threats and pummeled her into oblivion with a two-by-four?"

Obviously startled, Mickey looked up to see who had posed this loaded question. Seeing it was Biter, he started laughing. "What are you doing here?"

"I've come to offer you a job. I own a bar now—the Red Dragon on the Bayfront, and I'm looking for a cook. I was hoping you'd come to work for me. I'll pay you more than you're making here."

"Is this a joke? 'Cause, if it is, it ain't funny."

Biter looked Mickey in the eyes and said firmly, "No, it's no joke. I need a cook, and I would like to have you on my team... if you're interested."

"Why me?"

Biter hesitated momentarily as he pondered the question. "Truthfully, I don't know why. Whenever I try to think of someone I know who might be a good fit to fill this position, your face, for some reason, keeps coming into my head." Biter realized how absurd all this must sound to Mickey, and he started to laugh. "Do you even know how to cook?"

Mickey began to laugh as well. "Maybe that should have been your first question, but yeah, I do. You wouldn't know it by looking at my scrawny frame, but I love to eat, and I love to cook. I'm quite good at it, too, if I do say so myself."

Biter couldn't help himself and asked, "Which one?"

Mickey looked confused. "What?"

"Which one are you good at? Eating or cooking?"

Mickey started laughing. "You're still an ass! You know what I mean. Cooking, of course!"

Biter broke up laughing as well. "That's great! Look, I know it sounds crazy, but I really think this is a sign of some kind, and I think you coming to work for me would be a good move for both of us."

"How can you be sure I won't get stressed out and have another episode like before?"

Biter winced at the memory of what his thoughtless act had done to Mickey in the past. With genuine remorse, he said, "Because I will never put you in that position again. I give you my word that either me or another of my bartenders will always be on duty when you are working. I know I was an asshole and treated you badly. I don't blame you for questioning my motives now—that's just you being smart, but I really have changed. I wish you could believe me. If you take the job, you'll be doing me a favor. What do you say?"

Mickey hesitated for a minute. He desperately wanted to say yes, but he still feared that this was all a cruel joke. He looked Biter in the eyes to gauge his sincerity. "And you'll pay me more than I'm making here?"

"Yes, and you won't have to work nights. What do you say?"

Mickey broke into a smile. "I say when do I start, boss?"

Biter laughed heartily. "As soon as Zarenstein can find a replacement for you. I wouldn't want you to leave him in a lurch. My cook won't be leaving for a month yet, so if you can start in two weeks, there'll still be more than enough time for him to train you."

Mickey came around the end of the buffet table and gave Biter a big hug. Biter remembered the last time he and Mickey had embraced, and he profoundly regretted the circumstances that had led up to it. As Mickey now started to release his grasp, this time it was Biter who tightened his and continued the embrace for a while longer.

THIRTY-ONE

Biter was understandably apprehensive the first day Mickey reported for work at the Red Dragon. He was worried how his former co-worker would relate to the bartenders, and he was concerned that the regulars, with their propensity for uttering insensitive comments, might just drive him over the edge.

Biter knew his motivation to hire Mickey was well-intentioned—he wanted to help him move forward in his life—but he now feared that his decision to hire him might ultimately prove to have just the opposite effect, and he didn't want to be the unwitting agent that set this man back even further.

To Biter's relief, his fears proved unfounded. The retiring cook, Gus, took Mickey under his wing. Although they were decades apart in age, they both had served in the military, and the two men became fast friends. By the time Gus left, Mickey was comfortable in his position and was actually thriving in his new environment. His cooking was equally as good as his predecessor's, and the normally persnickety regulars voiced no complaints. More importantly, Mickey was beginning to display self-confidence and was starting to build a genuine rapport with the locals.

The business, from a financial standpoint, was also doing well. The bar was packed with customers most nights, and the daily receipts frequently exceeded projections. Biter could not have been more pleased. He promoted Carl to bar manager, and since it was close to Christmas, he gave everyone on the payroll a generous year-end bonus.

For the locals, he created a Pint Club with a prestigious sounding name—The Royal Order of the Red Dragon. All inductees had their names engraved on crystal mugs, which were then hug above the bar. JT was the first inductee and the only member of the club posthumously honored in this way. All mugs, except for his, were pointed toward the east. JT's alone faced west, toward the sea. Each Tuesday, the first bartender on duty would place a beer on the back of the bar under a picture of JT, and all members of the Club who came in that day would receive their first beer free. Over time, as a club member died, his or her mug would ceremoniously be turned to face the ocean as well.

To raise food for the local food bank, Biter initiated an ongoing program where customers who brought in non-perishable food items received a dollar off each beer they purchased that day. He also started sponsoring all of the high school sports teams in Newport and surrounding communities. Not surprisingly, word soon spread that he was an easy mark for a donation, and nearly every scout troop, church group, and nonprofit youth organization in the county sent a representative to the bar, looking for support. None were turned away empty-handed.

Rather than viewing these requests as an annoyance, Biter actually welcomed them and was grateful for the opportunity to give back to the local community in some small way. He knew that the events of the last six months had changed him. He no longer felt the need for the grand gesture to feed his ego and was content just being himself.

Mac noticed a change in Biter as well. He understood better than anyone how profoundly Biter had been affected by JT's death and had feared that his friend would never be able to fully recover from this traumatic event. He was, therefore, relieved to see this positive change in Biter's demeanor and was eager to accept it as a sign that he had underestimated his emotional resilience. He felt compelled to encourage Biter to stay on the new path he had chosen for himself and lingered late one Sunday evening so he would be the sole customer in the bar when Biter initiated his closing procedures.

As Biter began cleaning the grill, he looked over at Mac and said, "I know you need several warnings, but this really is last call."

"I'll take another beer," Mac replied. "There's no one else in the bar, and it's close to midnight. Why don't you lock the front door, get one for yourself and join me?"

Biter sighed heavily, lowered his head and threw the pumice block he was using to clean the grill to the side. He walked to the front door, locked it and then went to the taps, poured two pounders and passed one to Mac. "This beer's on the house. So why are you here so late?"

"Oh, for fuck's sake, why do I have to have a reason to have a beer with my favorite bartender?"

Biter snorted, "Come on, give me a break."

"OK, I and just about everyone else who comes into this bar on a regular basis has noticed a change in you."

Biter became defensive. "So what's your point?"

Mac held up his hands. "No, no, don't get your back up. It's a positive thing," he chuckled. "How do I say this without offending you? You're not your dickish self anymore."

"Wow, thanks for the high praise," Biter said facetiously.

Mac chortled. "No, I was just kidding. Don't get me wrong, you have always had your good qualities, but sometimes they have been overshadowed by the negative facets of your personality. Nobody's perfect, we all have our flaws. I just wanted you to know that I and the boys wholeheartedly approve of the change we've seen in you. It's like you've molted and grown into a nicer you."

Biter looked confused. "Molted?"

"I thought you were a marine biologist? You know, like a Dungeness crab. You've molted and shed your dickish self. You're truly a nice guy now, Biter."

"Did you just call me Biter?"

Mac smiled. "Well, that's your name, isn't it?"

Biter laughed heartily. "What happened to Ray?"

Mac tried to keep from laughing, but couldn't help himself. "He was the dickish side of your personality—the last molt."

Biter chuckled. "Mac, only you could take a compliment and make it sound like a put down but thanks just the same. I appreciate the attaboy, especially coming from you."

Mac became serious. "The change I see in you would suggest that your decision to buy the bar was the right one for you. I just wanted to be sure you haven't had any second thoughts."

"No, it feels right. Mai always said we were all just one big family. We may be a little dysfunctional at times, but we are a family just the same. I have no regrets."

"Well, that's music to my ears, son." Mac chugged the last of his beer and got off his stool. "I better get home before the missus starts to think I'm cheating on her."

"And I better get back to cleaning the grill," Biter replied. He downed the rest of his beer and walked Mac to the front door. Unlocking it, he turned to his friend and patted him on the shoulder. "You're a good guy too, Mac…for a lawyer that is."

Mac smiled as he walked through the door. Biter watched him cross the parking lot to his car. "No, seriously, Mac," he yelled. "Thanks for your friendship and tell the guys thanks as well."

"I will, son. Have a good evening. I'll see you tomorrow at the usual time."

Biter locked the front door and resumed his closing chores.

THIRTY-TWO

By the time Biter returned home he was dead tired and eager to get some sleep. He walked upstairs to his bedroom, undressed quickly and turned the light switch off next to his bed before hopping in the sack. Pulling the covers over him, he glanced at the clock on his nightstand. Its illuminated face was the only muted light in the otherwise jet black room. It was 2 a.m.

As soon as Biter closed his eyes, he heard strange noises outside the house, which were followed shortly thereafter by loud, very deliberate footsteps, coming from his downstairs living room. His heart rate quickened, and he jumped up in bed, fearing there was an intruder in the house!

Before Biter could get out of bed, the room became engulfed in an intense white light, and he collapsed back down on the mattress awestruck and unable to move. Although the light was incredibly brilliant, it was not blinding. Rather than having to avert his eyes, Biter felt compelled to stare directly into the light and lay transfixed on the bed, his eyes wide open.

He also felt no increase in body temperature as he would have if he were being bathed in direct sunlight. Instead he felt a more soothing and subtle warmth—one of an emotional and spiritual nature. The pure white light was all comforting and all loving.

Biter noticed there was a cloud of energy swirling silently, like a benevolent swarm of bees, near the ceiling on the far side of the room above two framed pictures of JT. He guessed that this energy cloud was the source of this intense white light.

He felt his chest compress as if he was being given a big, loving bear hug, and he instinctively sensed that this was a visit from JT and that his departed friend had transitioned to another realm. An energy field suddenly engulfed him, and the energy instantly enervated and activated his entire being. Every hair on his body was erect and awake. Each and every cell in his body tingled with electrical excitement. He could feel the energy coursing through his veins. The feeling was incredible, and he never felt so alive in his life! An overwhelming sense of well-being overtook him, and he knew unconditional love. He lost all sense of time. It was sheer bliss!

He savored the experience and longed fervently for it to continue unabated forever but knew sadly it would not. He sensed somehow this was JT's farewell—it was his dear friend saying, "Good bye...for now."

Without warning, the energy source left his body, the hovering cloud instantly disappeared and the room was once again cloaked in pitch black darkness. As Biter lay on the bed, his body still shaking with excitement, he realized that JT had given him the greatest gift possible—the firm belief that there was, indeed, an afterlife and that he would be reunited with his friend again upon his death. The enormity of this insight overwhelmed him, and he began to cry uncontrollably. Realizing he had no idea how much time had transpired, he looked at the clock on his nightstand. It was 2:40 a.m. He closed his eyes but couldn't sleep and lay awake for hours, reliving the experience. Finally, just before dawn, exhaustion overtook his overactive mind, and he drifted off into a deep sleep.

At noon, Biter was awakened by the incessant ringing of his downstairs telephone. As he fumbled his way out of bed and headed down the stairs, he heard the unmistakable electronic voice of his answering machine directing the caller to leave a message. Although the volume was too low for him to discern the words spoken, he thought he recognized the caller's voice, but so much had happened the night before, he questioned whether he was just dreaming.

When he finally got to the phone, he saw the blinking red light on the answering machine, depressed the message button, and waited anxiously to determine the identity of the caller. As soon as the message commenced, he knew he hadn't been dreaming. The caller was his old girlfriend, Cassandra.

By the shakiness of her voice, he could tell she was obviously stressed. "Biter, I've been in Europe on an art internship for the past year and just heard the terrible news. Is it true? Oh God, I hope it's not! I'm afraid to say what it is for fear that by saying it, I might make it so. I loved JT as much as you did."

There was a long pause, and then Biter heard her sobbing. "No, I'm sorry. That's not possible. You and JT were closer than brothers. You must be devastated."

After another long pause, she said, "I know you. You must be a mess! I want to come down this weekend and spend time with you…if you think it would be OK. I still love you and can't bear to see you in pain. Please call me."

Tears streamed down Biter's face. He knew it had been over two years since his break up with Cassandra and questioned whether it was even possible for them to get back together after all that had happened in the interim. He knew he had changed. He didn't know whether she had and, if so, in what way, but he felt compelled to find out. For some reason, the prospect of change, or maybe commitment, no longer scared him. He dialed her number. After three unanswered rings, he was getting ready to put down the phone when he heard her pick up.

AFTERWORD

Eight months after my best friend's death, I traveled to Mesquite, Nevada to visit his mother and observe what would have been his 36th birthday. Two days later, I went to Las Vegas and met up with my old friend Pastor Doug, whom I had not seen in several years and who was then living with his wife and kids in San Diego. Doug and I had been friends for years. I met him when he was just a college student, and this was long before he decided to make the ministry his life's work. It was Doug who introduced me to my dear friend, the person who was the inspiration for this book.

After a few drinks in the bar at the Monte Carlo, I, for some reason, decided to open up and share with Doug the amazing events I had experienced in the months after our mutual friend's death. Up until that time, I hadn't told anyone these stories for fear that the person I told them to would either think I was crazy or assume I was so overtaken with grief that I was just hallucinating. With Doug, this was not a concern. I knew he would be more open-minded and caring. As I shared my stories with him, he just sat there silently, not saying anything. I remember thinking at the time that it was odd that he didn't seem to be taken aback by the seemingly outlandish stories I was recounting. When I finished, I said, "You don't seem surprised by what I've just told you."

Doug smiled knowingly and said, "Biter, I hear stories like yours all the time. I think the purpose of this trip is for me to tell you to write down your experiences."

When I got home, I started to keep a journal and had no intention of sharing it with anyone, except, perhaps, with Doug, as a parting gift upon my death. However, life has a way of changing the best-laid plans. I took a job at a museum in Tacoma, Washington, which is nearly 300 miles from my home in Tidewater, Oregon, and began commuting back and forth each week by train. To occupy my time, I started writing, and after nearly six years, the product of my effort is before you.

This book has been an amazing journey for me personally, and I feel like the narrative has taken on a life of its own. It was always meant to be a celebration of my friend's life and the profound effect he had on my spiritual development, but it was originally envisioned as a fairly straightforward, autobiographical account of my experiences.

This book is not that. It is a work of fiction, and the story is far more elaborate than what I had set down to write. I feel as if my departed friend has guided my hand in so many passages in this book that he should legitimately be given co-author status for this work. Not knowing who wrote what, I'll just acknowledge his contribution here and thank my eternal friend for the inspiration he provided.

Greg Starypan
Fall 2013

Greg Starypan claims the Pacific Northwest as home; although he was born in New Jersey, he has lived in either Oregon or Washington State for the past thirty-eight years. Graduating from the University of Washington with a BS in oceanography and from Rutgers University with an MS in zoology, his professional career has included an interesting variety of jobs. Over the years, Starypan has worked as a researcher, community college instructor, aquaculture facility manager, zoo education director, grant writer, and acting animal curator.

Made in United States
Troutdale, OR
08/24/2025

Made in United States
Troutdale, OR
08/24/2025